To Remember What You've Read,
Write Your Initials in a Square.

DATE DUE

9/18/14	

OTTO'S
ORANGE DAY

JAY LYNCH & FRANK CAMMUSO

Visit us at www.abdopublishing.com

Reinforced library bound editions published in 2014 by Spotlight, a division of the ABDO Group, PO Box 398166, Minneapolis, MN 55439. Spotlight produces high-quality reinforced library bound editions for schools and libraries. Published by agreement with Raw Junior, LLC.

Printed in the United States of America, North Mankato, Minnesota.
042013
092013
This book contains at least 10% recycled material.

For Ngoc -*Frank*

For Kathleen and Norah -*Jay*

Editorial Director: FRANÇOISE MOULY
Advisor: ART SPIEGELMAN

Book Design: FRANÇOISE MOULY & JONATHAN BENNETT

A TOON BOOK

Library of Congress Cataloging-in-Publication Data
This book was previously cataloged with the following information:

Cammuso, Frank.
Otto's orange day / Frank Cammuso & Jay Lynch.
p. cm. -- (TOON Books)
Summary: After a genie fulfills Otto the cat's wish by turning the whole world orange, Otto realizes that his favorite color is not the best color for everything.
[1. Graphic novels. 2. Orange (Color) --Fiction. 3. Color --Fiction. 4. Cats --Fiction.]
PZ7.7.C36 Ot 2008
[E]

2007941868

ISBN 978-1-61479-154-6 (reinforced library bound edition)

Spotlight

All Spotlight books are reinforced library bindings and manufactured in the United States of America.

OTTO'S
ORANGE DAY

A TOON BOOK BY
JAY LYNCH & FRANK CAMMUSO
AN IMPRINT OF CANDLEWICK PRESS

CHAPTER ONE:

MY FAVORITE COLOR!

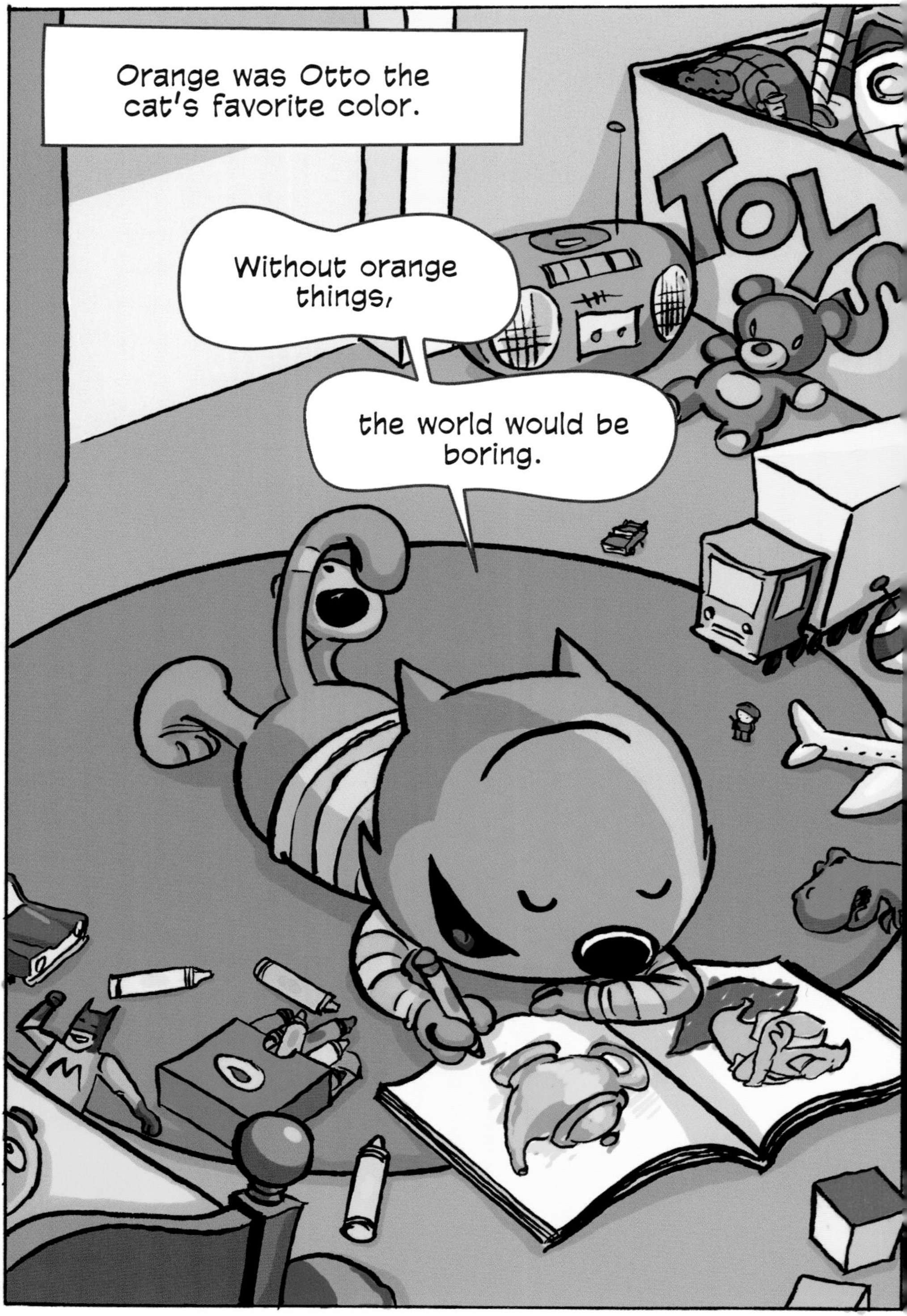
Orange was Otto the cat's favorite color.
Without orange things,
the world would be boring.
TOYS

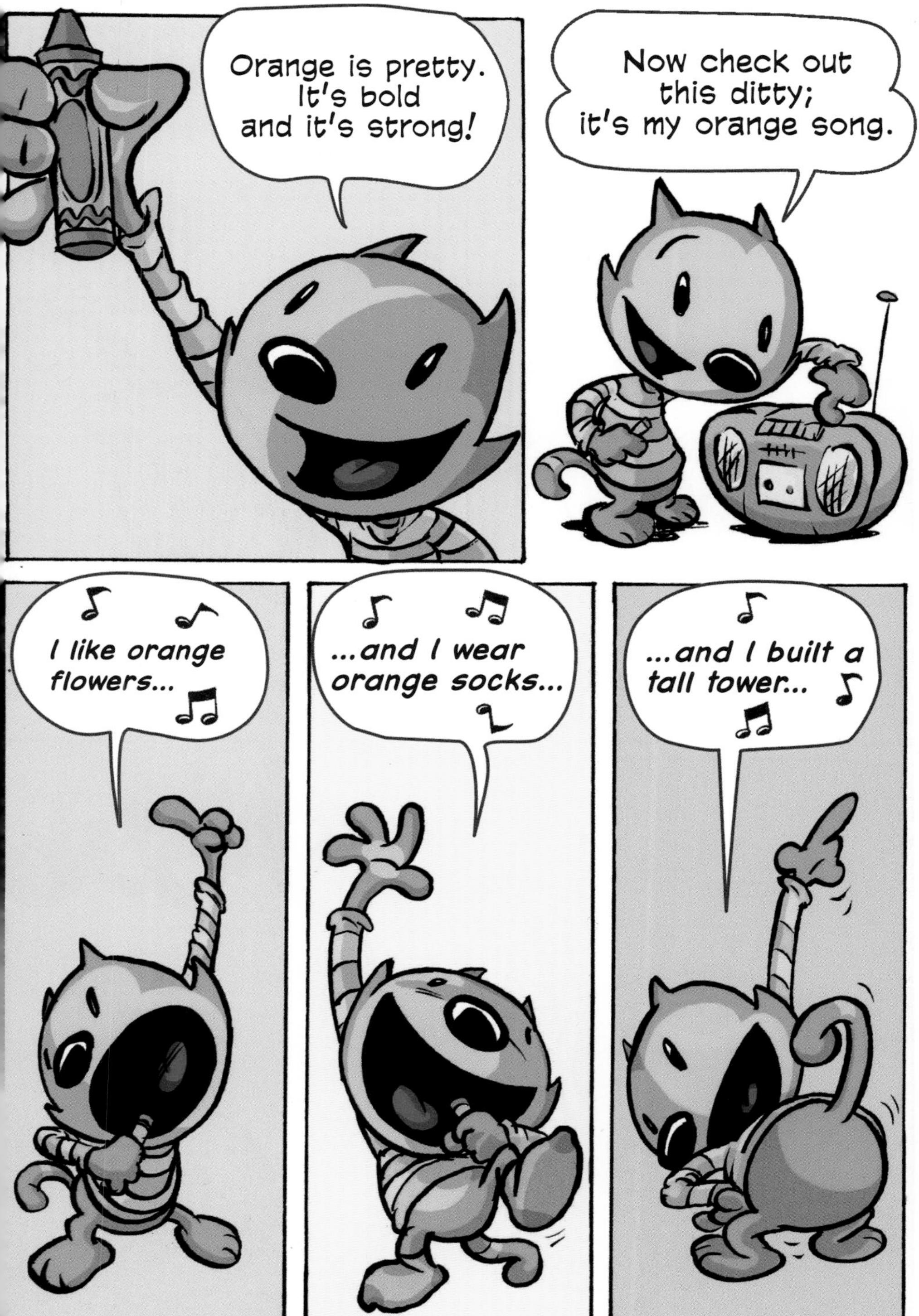
Orange is pretty. It's bold and it's strong!
Now check out this ditty; it's my orange song.
I like orange flowers...
...and I wear orange socks...
...and I built a tall tower...

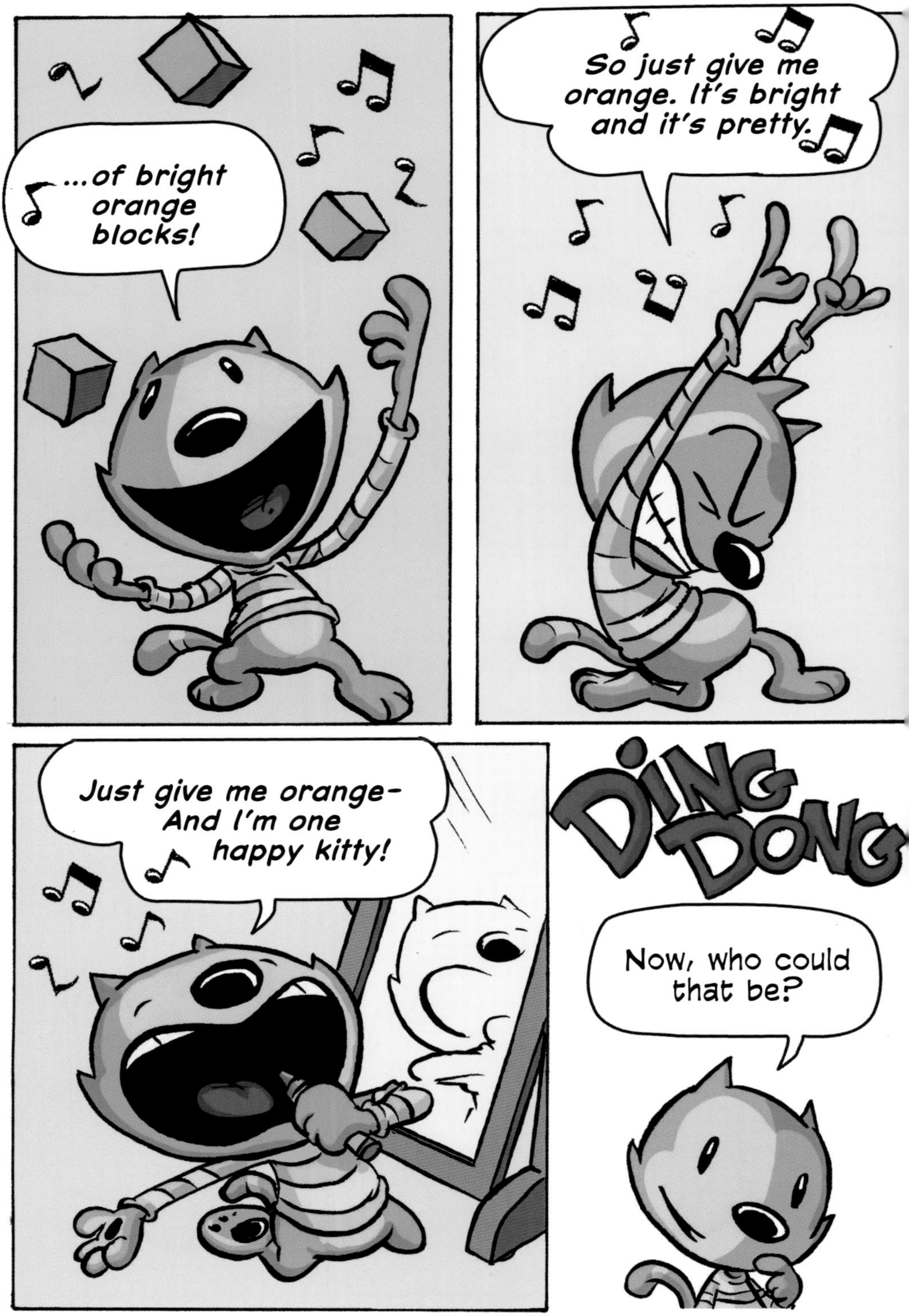
...of bright orange blocks!
So just give me orange. It's bright and it's pretty.
Just give me orange-
And I'm one happy kitty!
DING DONG
Now, who could that be?

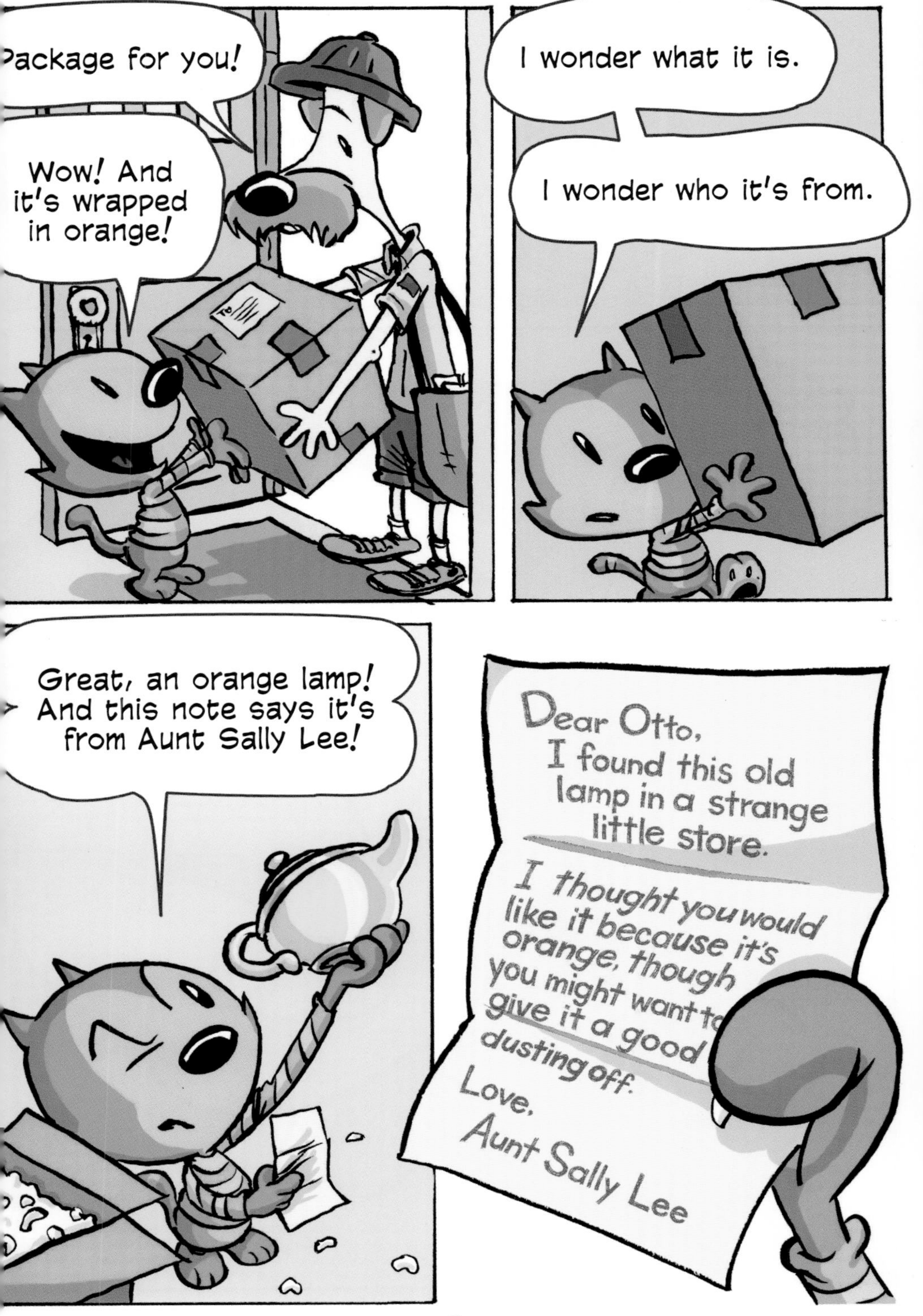
Package for you!
Wow! And it's wrapped in orange!
I wonder what it is.
I wonder who it's from.
Great, an orange lamp! And this note says it's from Aunt Sally Lee!
Dear Otto, I found this old lamp in a strange little store.
I thought you would like it because it's orange, though you might want to give it a good dusting off.
Love, Aunt Sally Lee

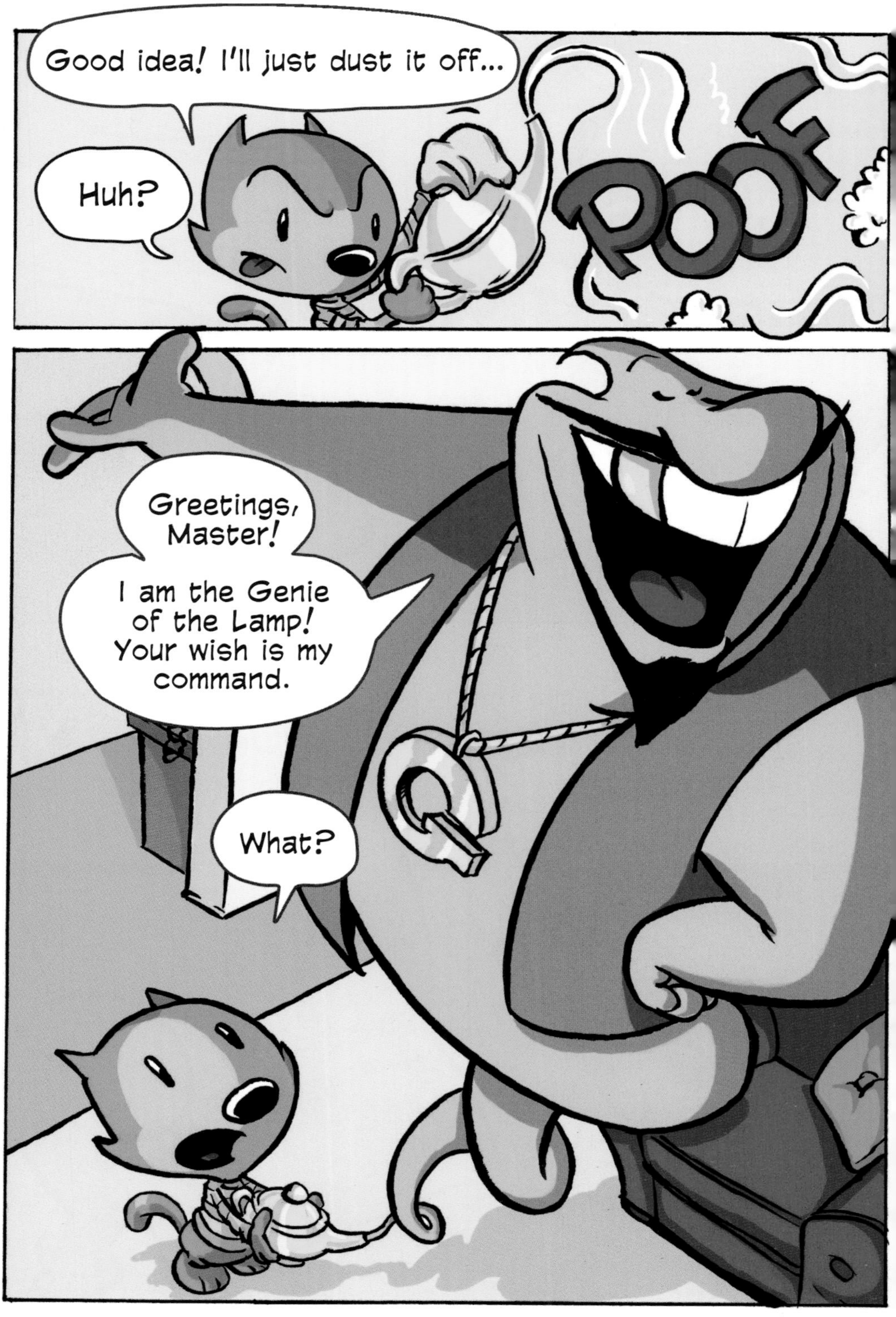
Good idea! I'll just dust it off...
Huh?
POOF
Greetings, Master!
I am the Genie of the Lamp! Your wish is my command.
What?

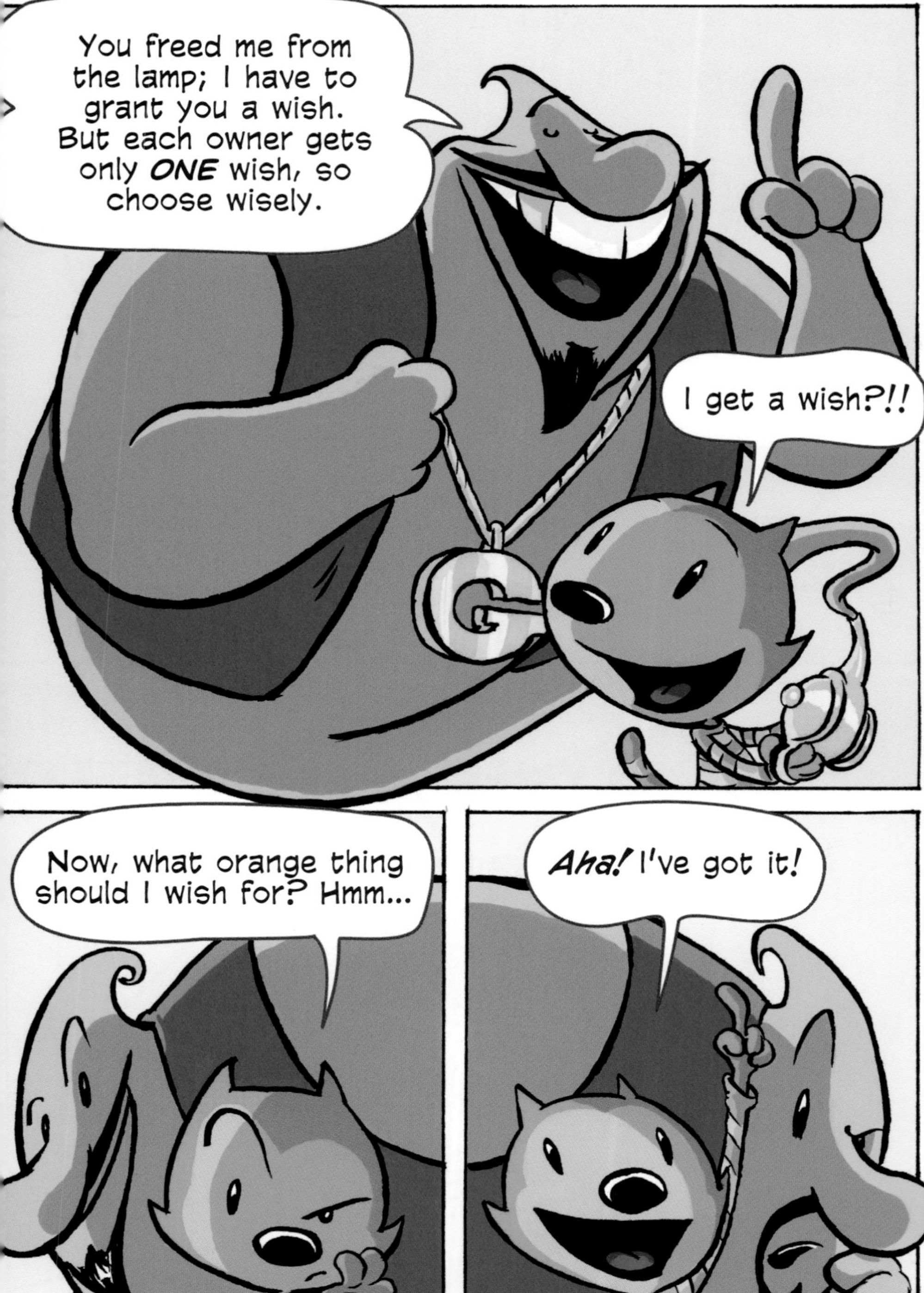
You freed me from the lamp; I have to grant you a wish. But each owner gets only *ONE* wish, so choose wisely.
I get a wish?!!
Now, what orange thing should I wish for? Hmm...
Aha! I've got it!

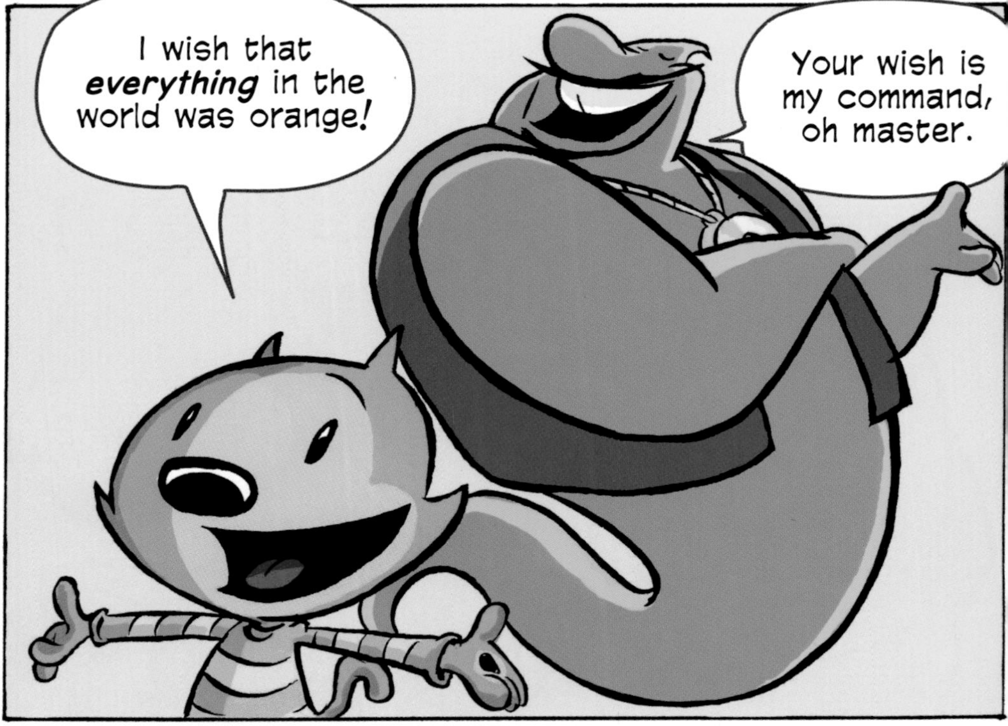
I wish that *everything* in the world was orange!
Your wish is my command, oh master.

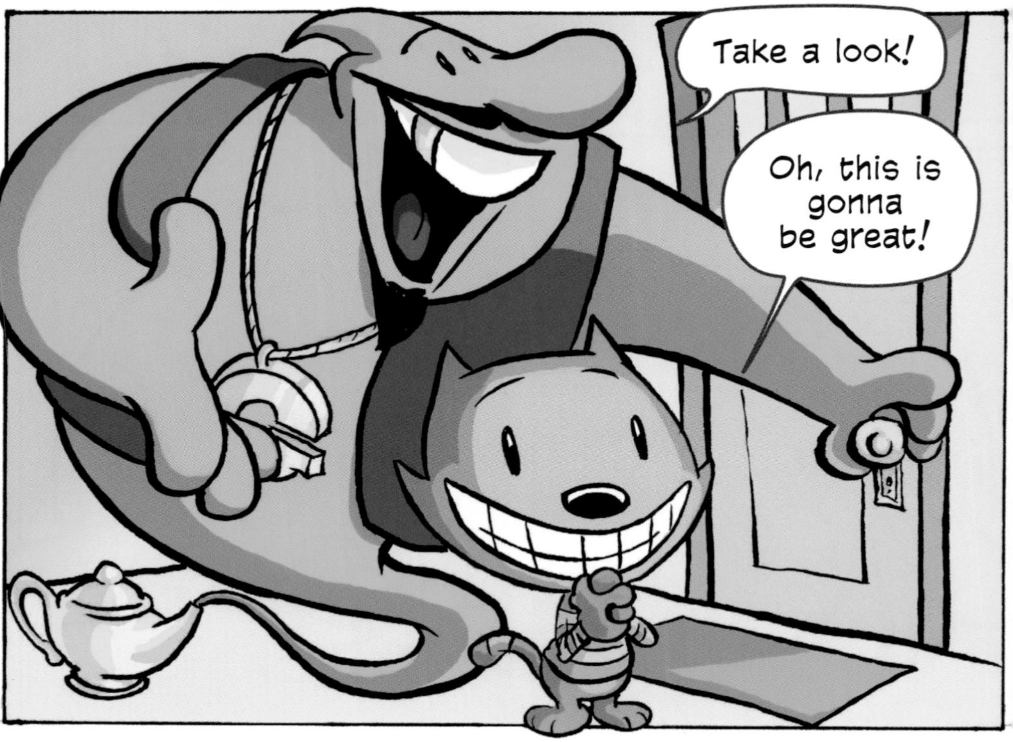
Take a look!
Oh, this is gonna be great!

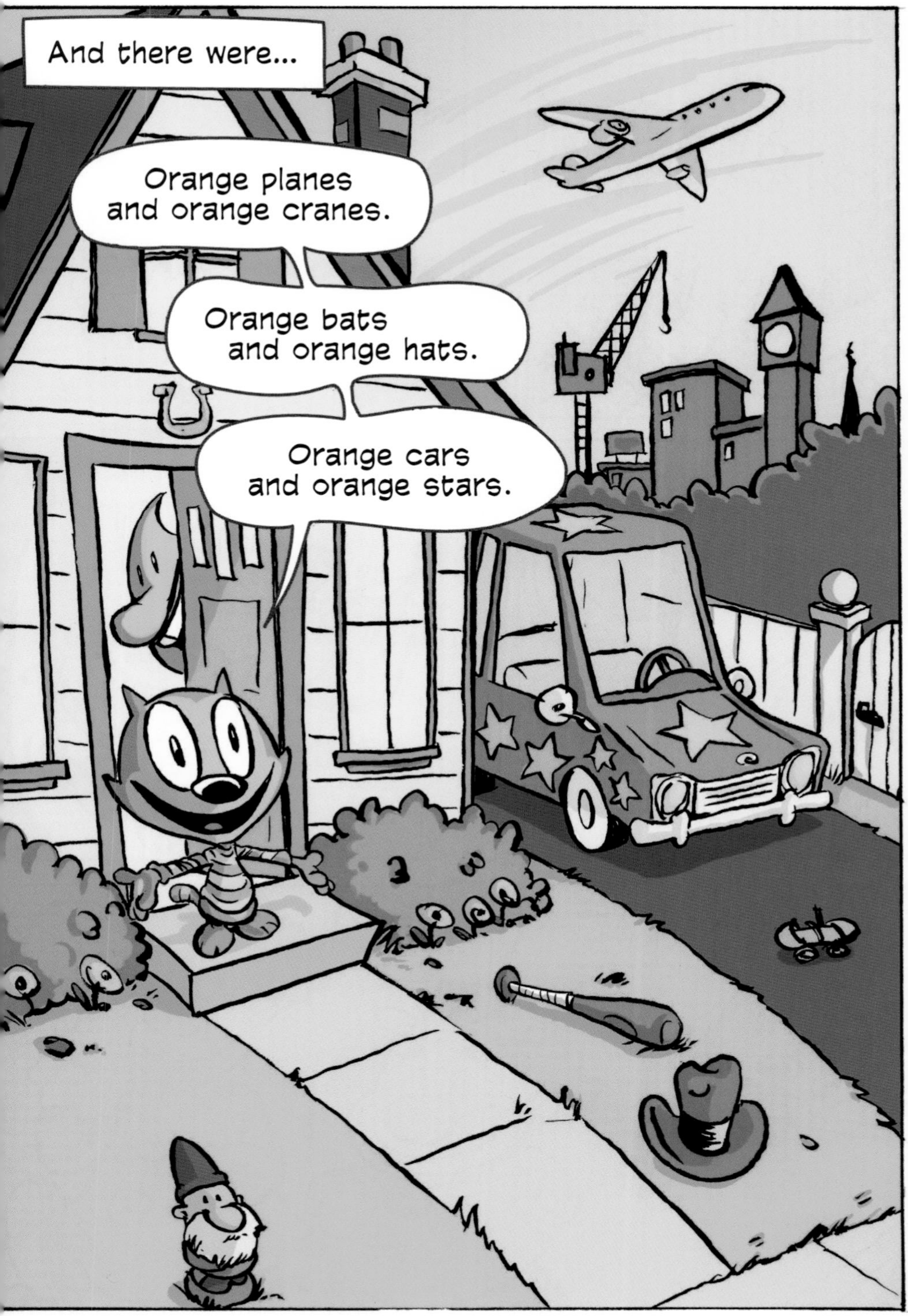
And there were...
Orange planes and orange cranes.
Orange bats and orange hats.
Orange cars and orange stars.

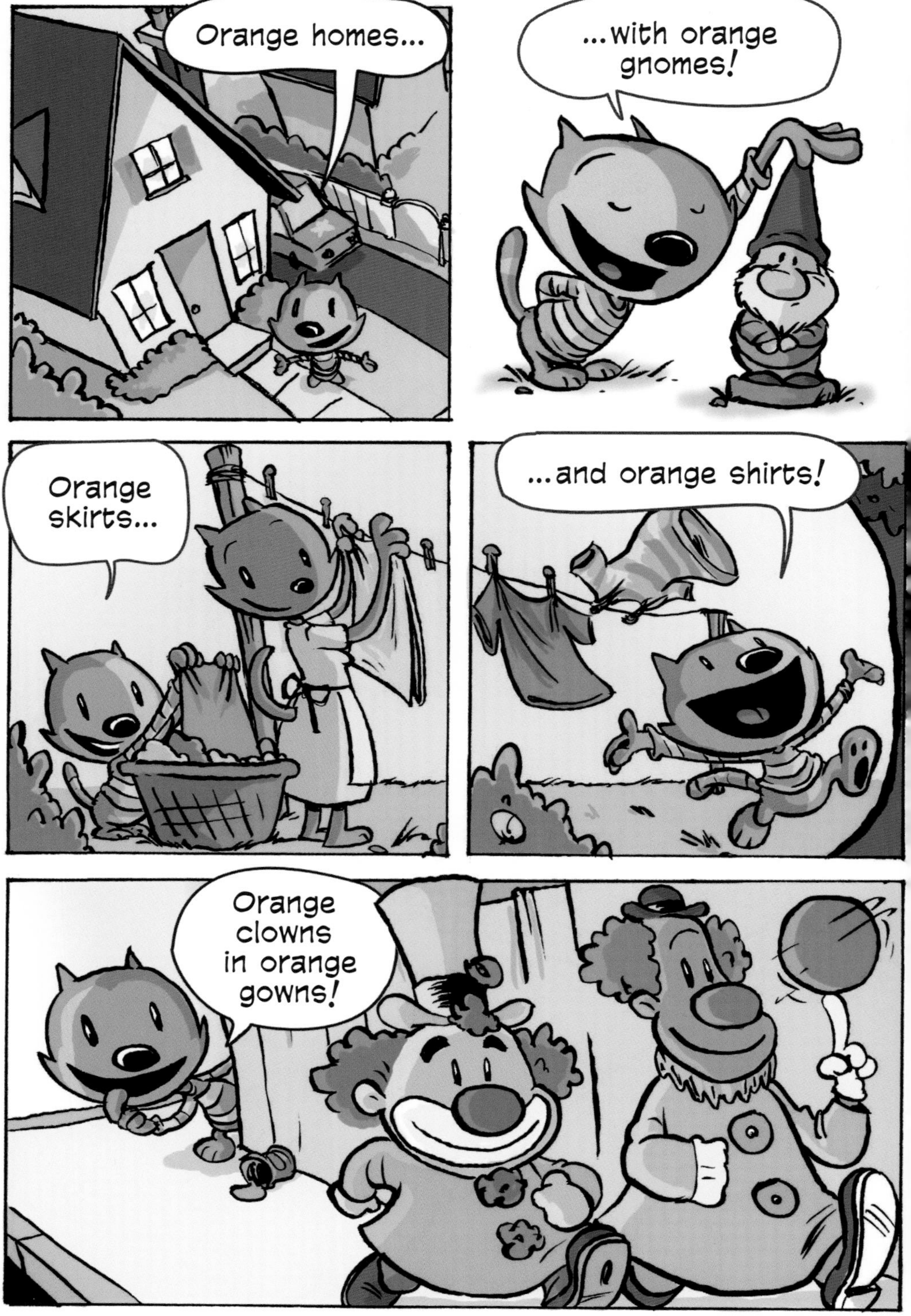
Orange homes...
...with orange gnomes!
Orange skirts...
...and orange shirts!
Orange clowns in orange gowns!

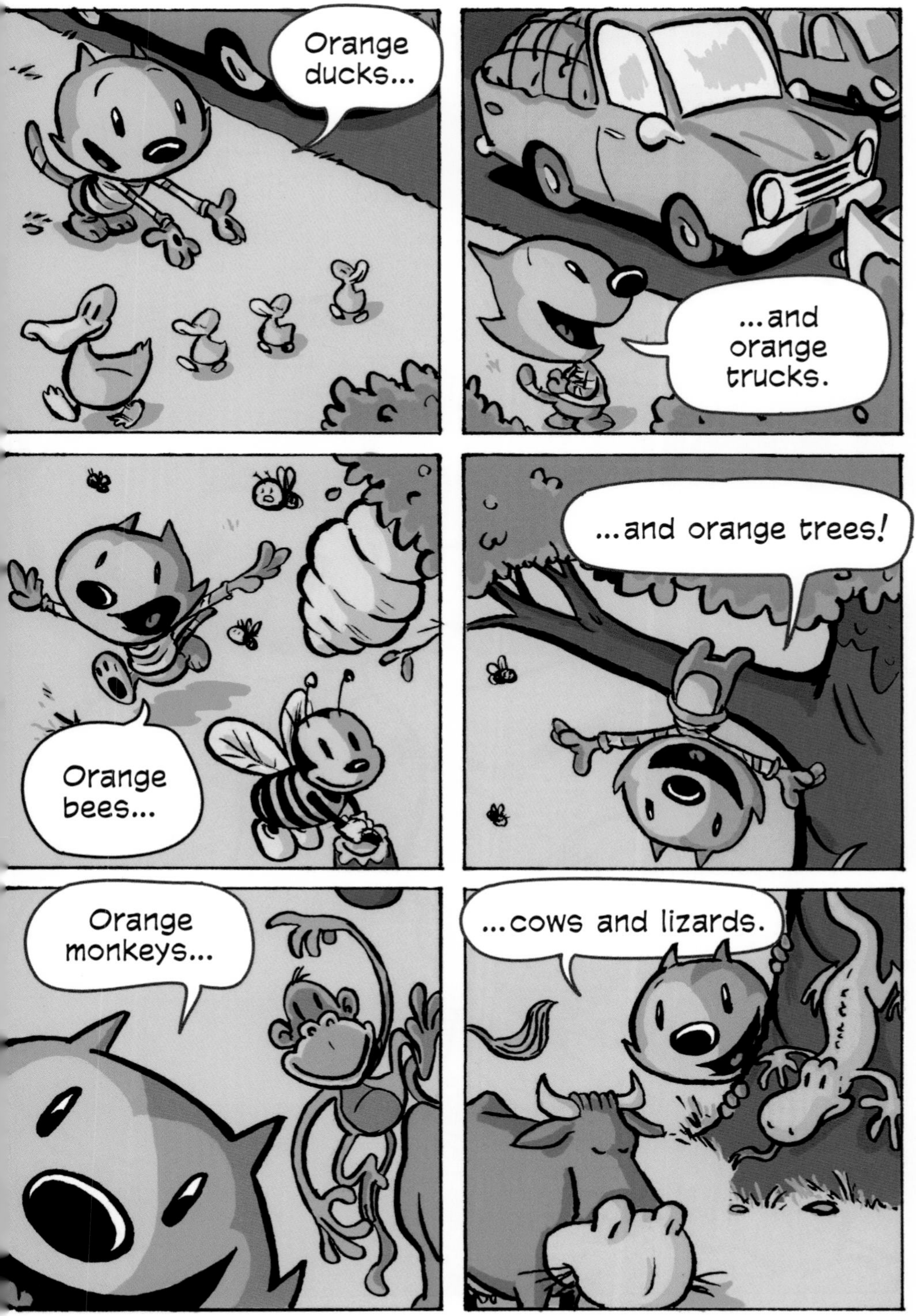
Orange ducks...
...and orange trucks.
Orange bees...
...and orange trees!
Orange monkeys...
...cows and lizards.

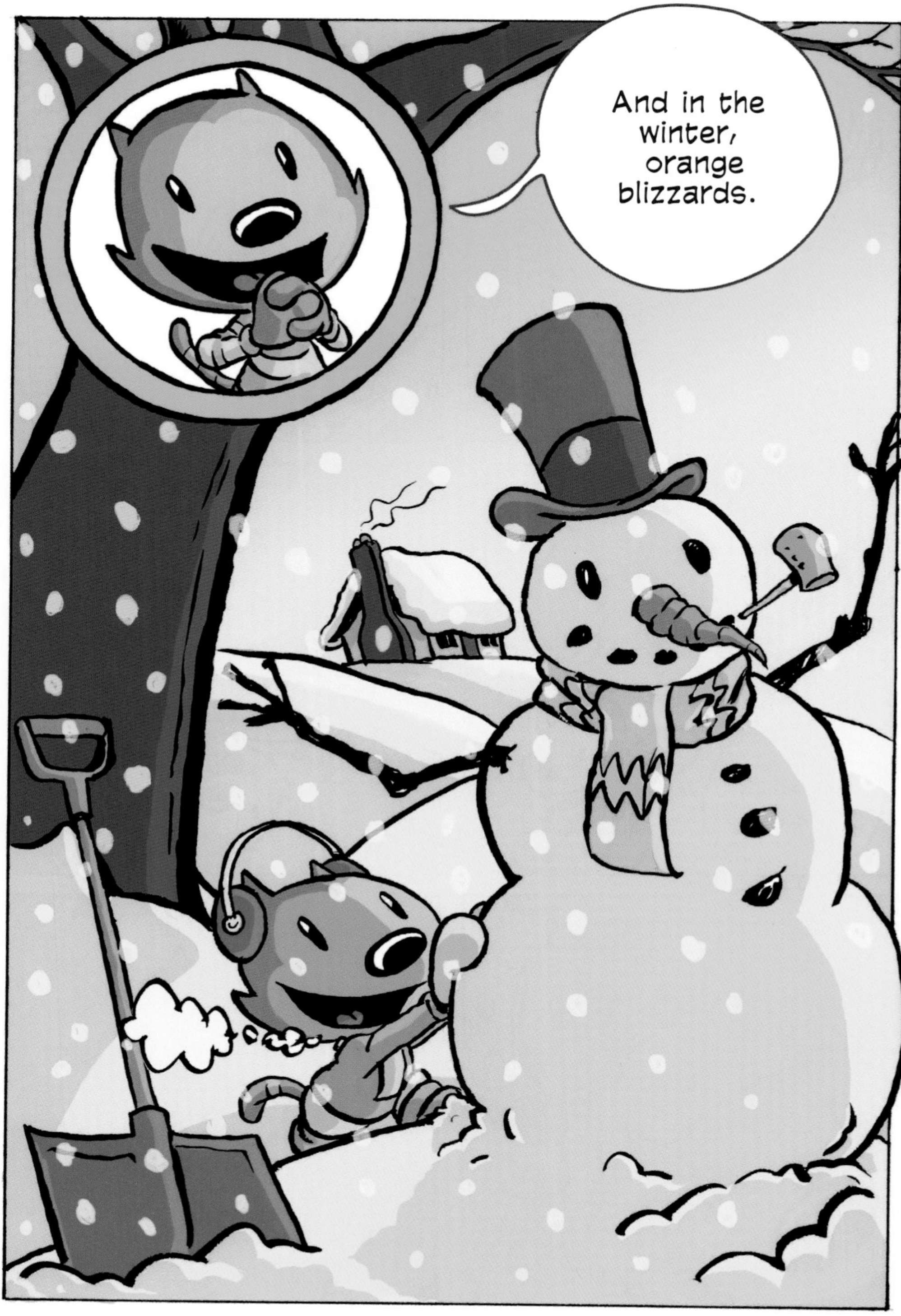
And in the winter, orange blizzards.

CHAPTER TWO:

BE CAREFUL WHAT YOU WISH FOR!

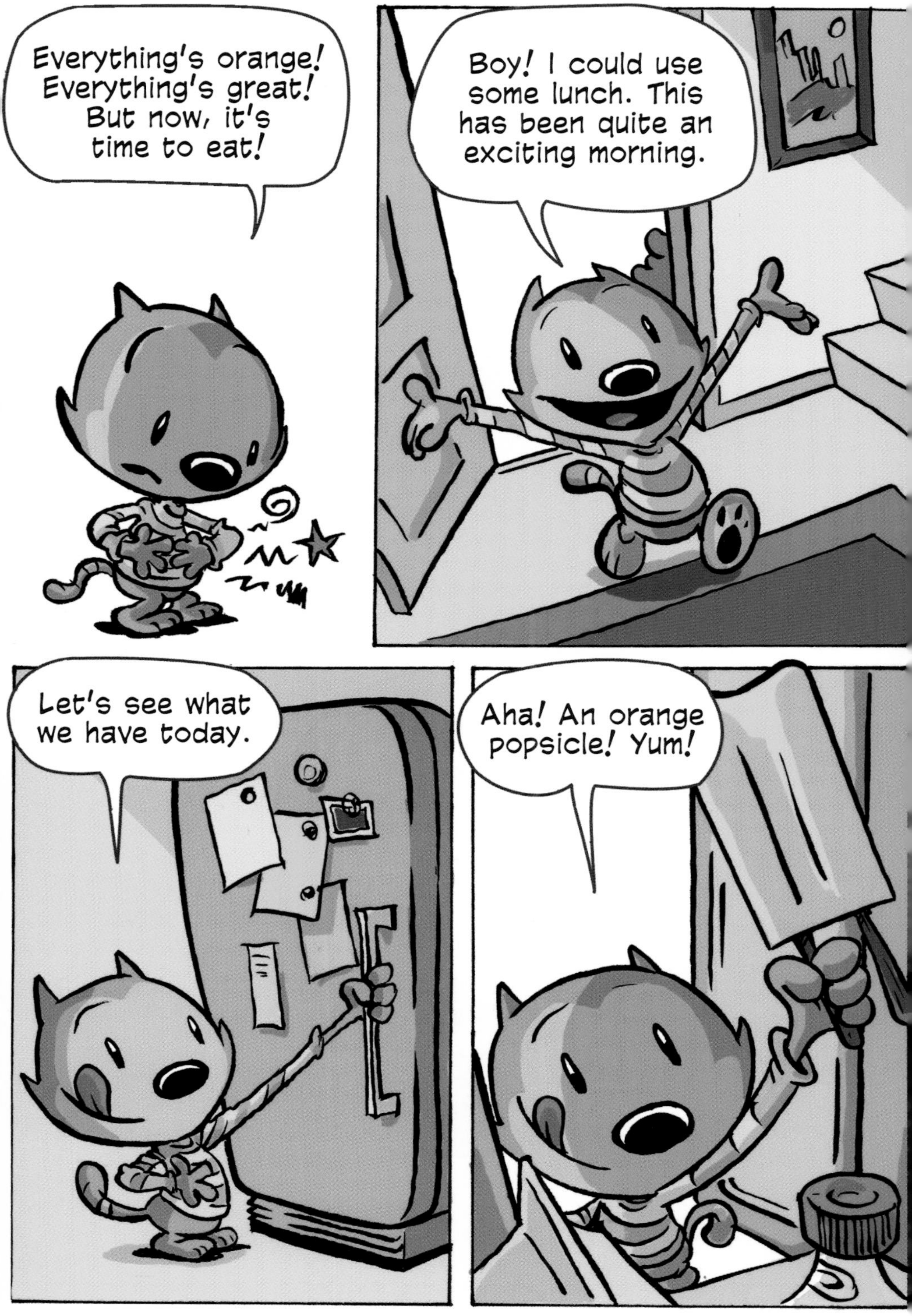
Everything's orange! Everything's great! But now, it's time to eat!
Boy! I could use some lunch. This has been quite an exciting morning.
Let's see what we have today.
Aha! An orange popsicle! Yum!

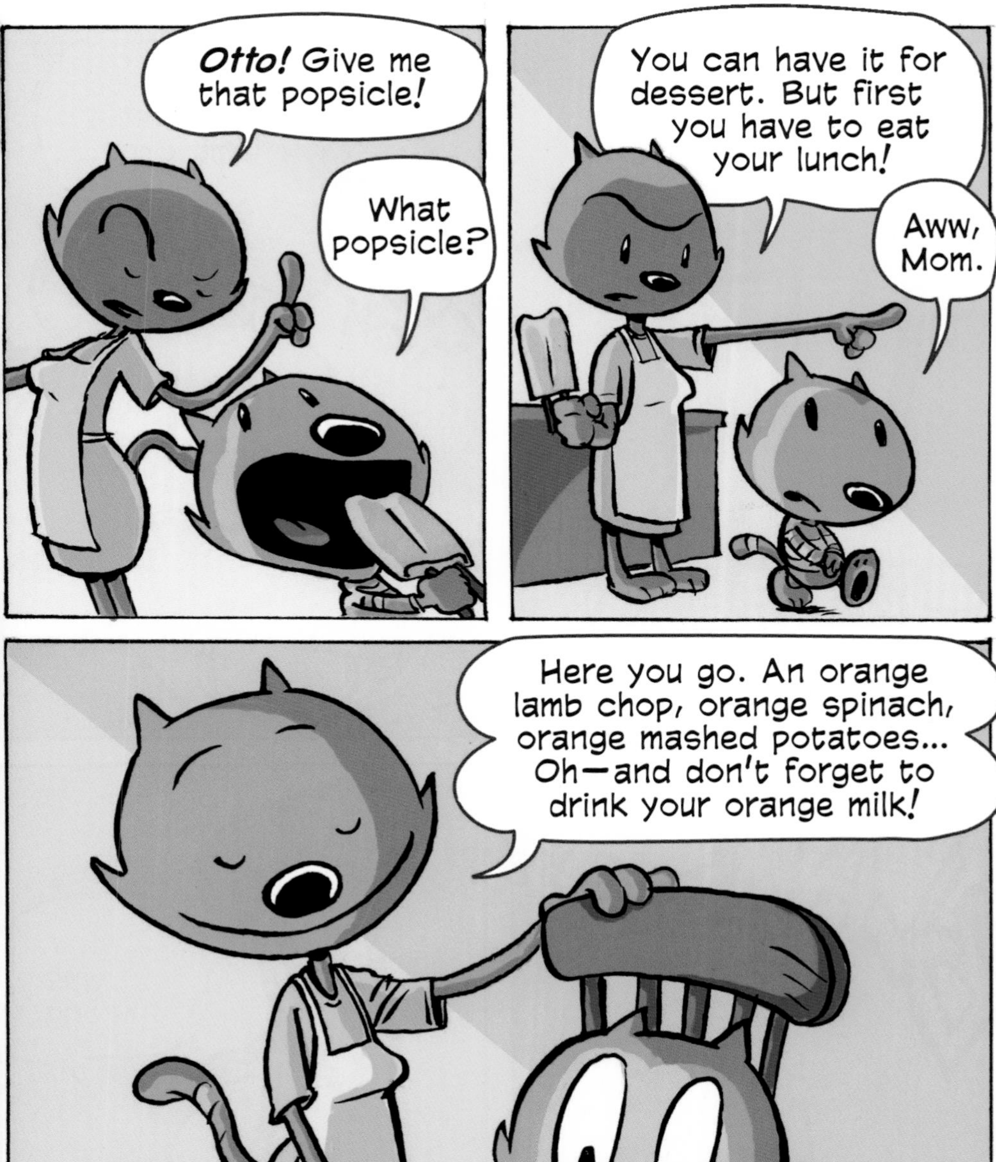
Otto! Give me that popsicle!
What popsicle?
You can have it for dessert. But first you have to eat your lunch!
Aww, Mom.
Here you go. An orange lamb chop, orange spinach, orange mashed potatoes... Oh—and don't forget to drink your orange milk!

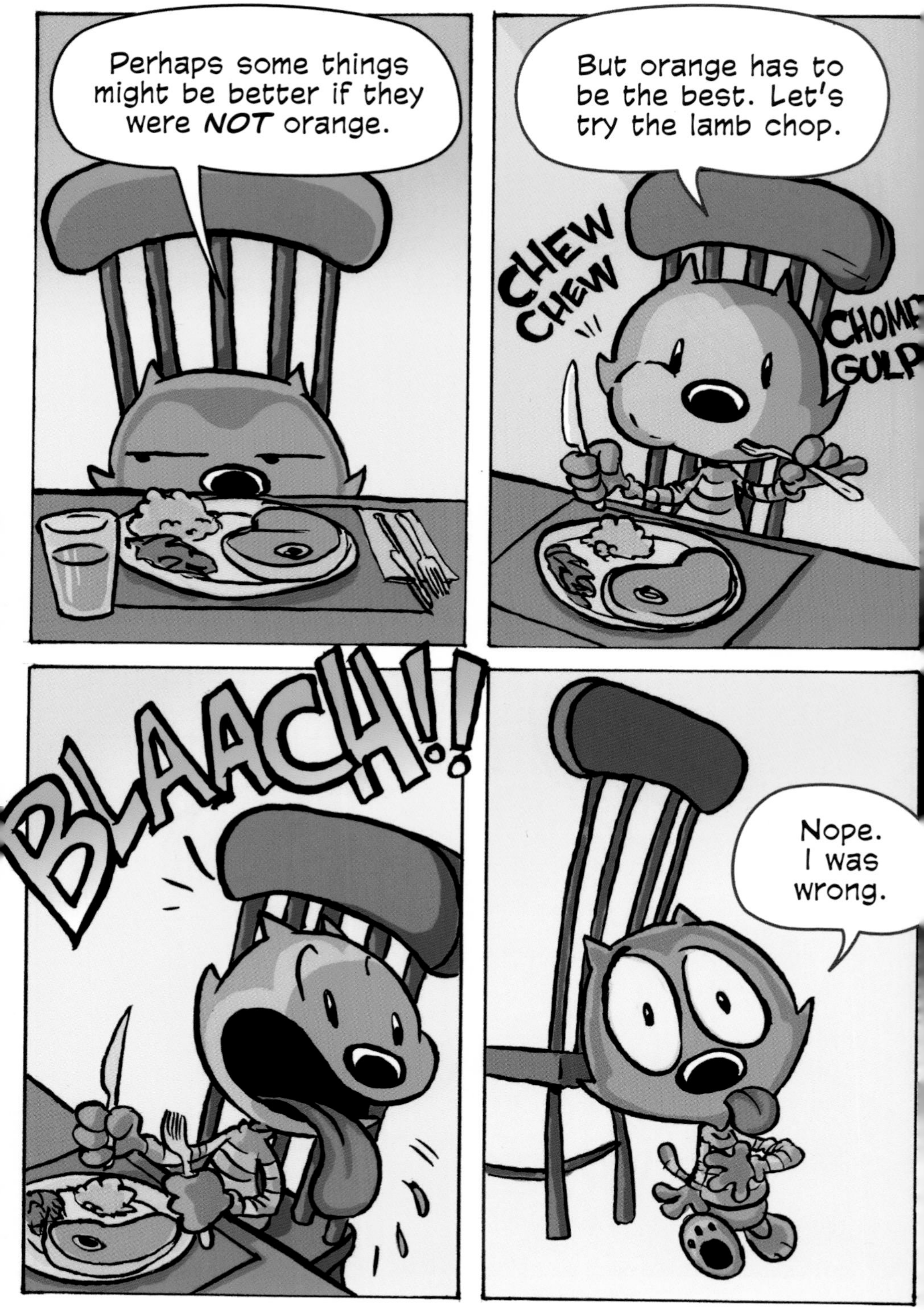
Perhaps some things might be better if they were NOT orange.
But orange has to be the best. Let's try the lamb chop.
CHEW CHEW
CHOMP GULP
BLAACH!!
Nope. I was wrong.

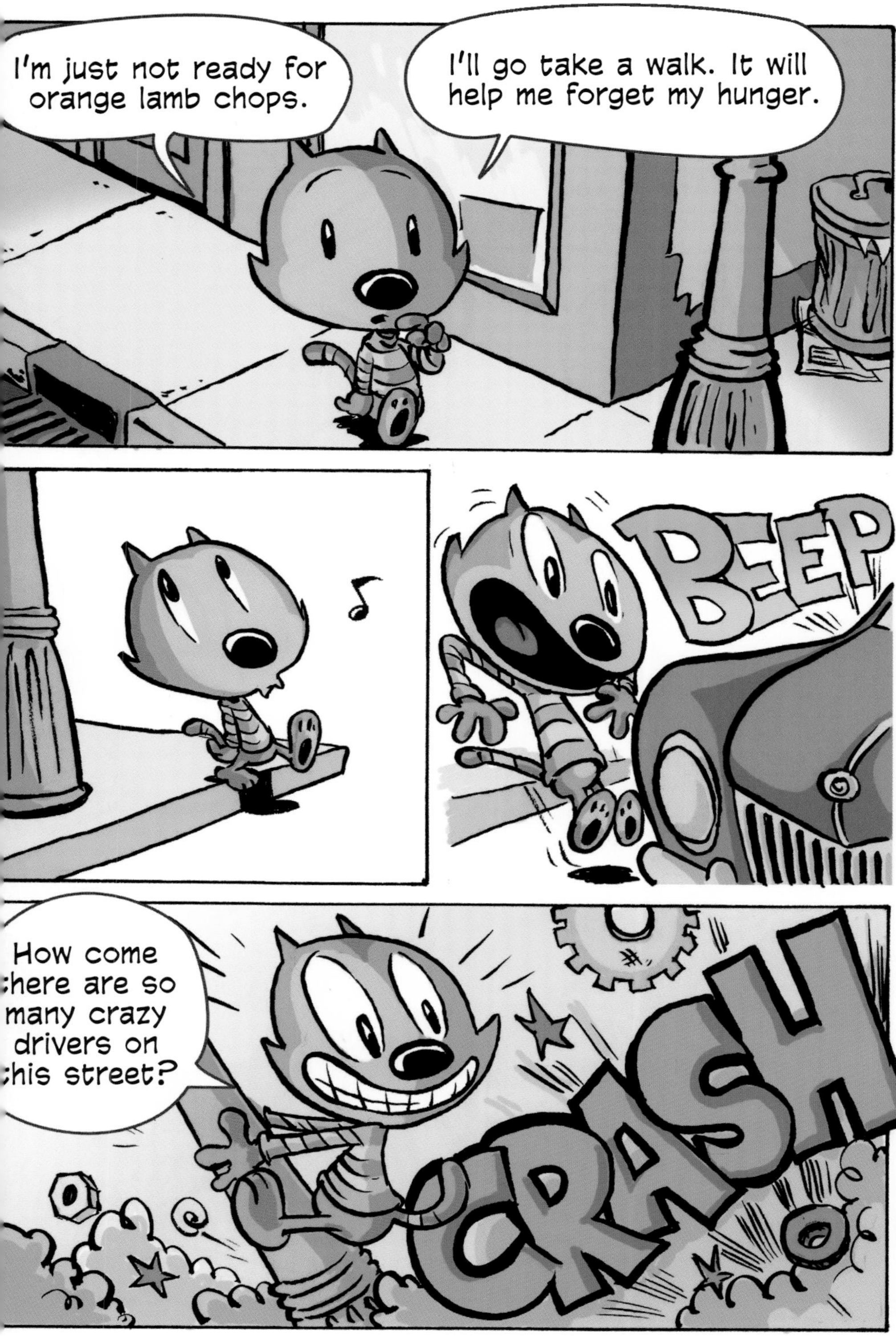
I'm just not ready for orange lamb chops.
I'll go take a walk. It will help me forget my hunger.
BEEP
How come here are so many crazy drivers on his street?
CRASH

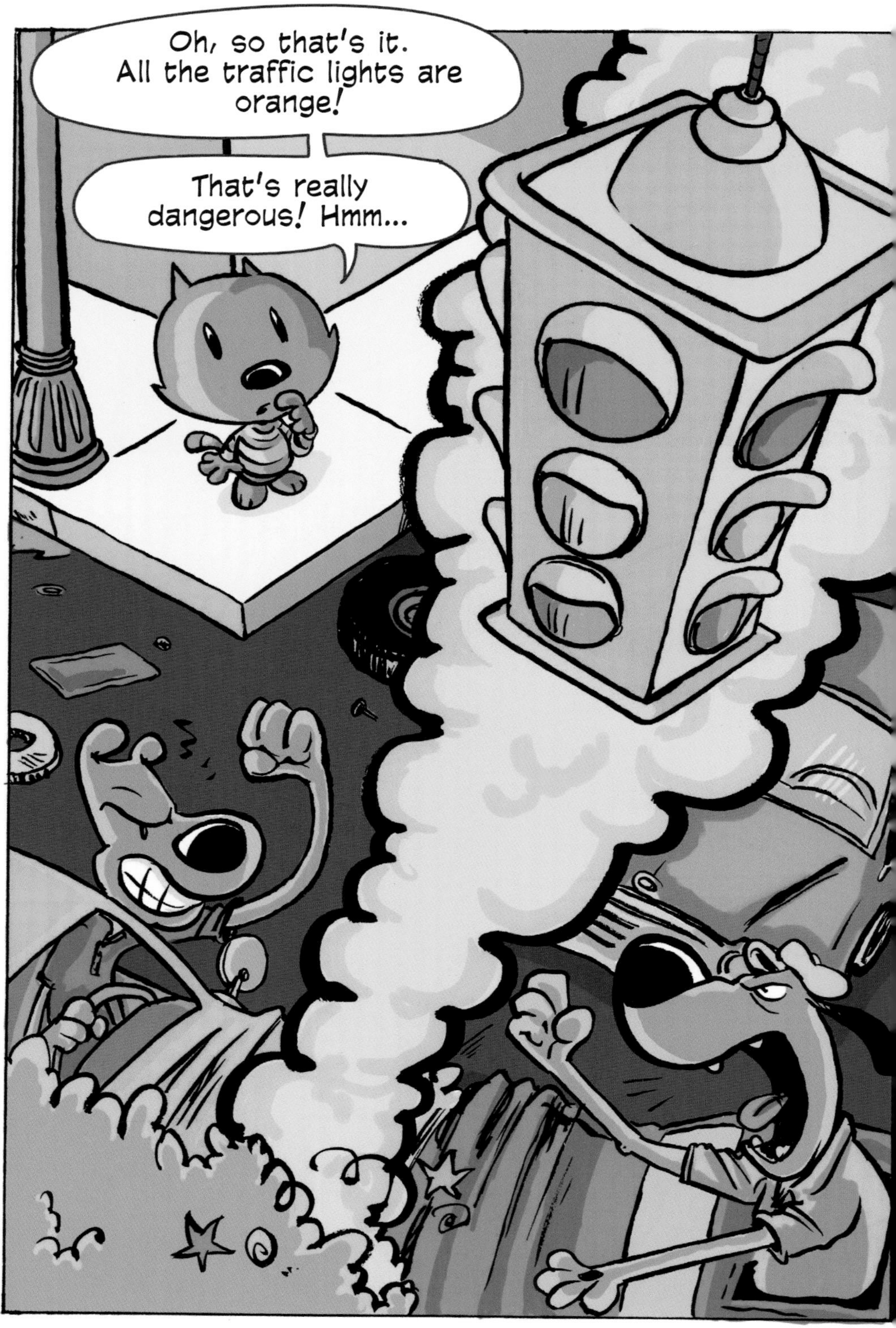
Oh, so that's it. All the traffic lights are orange!
That's really dangerous! Hmm...

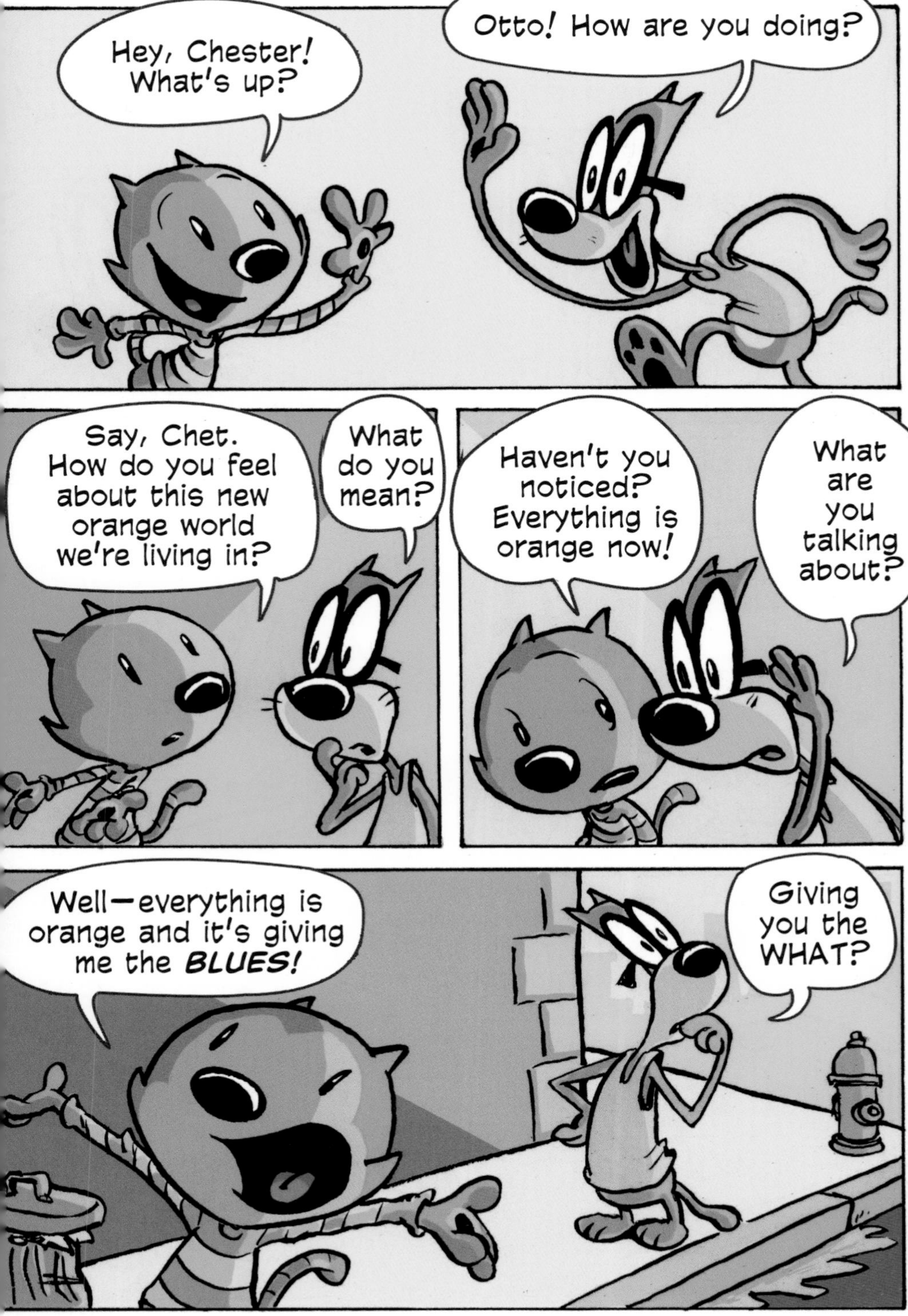
Hey, Chester! What's up?
Otto! How are you doing?
Say, Chet. How do you feel about this new orange world we're living in?
What do you mean?
Haven't you noticed? Everything is orange now!
What are you talking about?
Well—everything is orange and it's giving me the *BLUES!*
Giving you the WHAT?

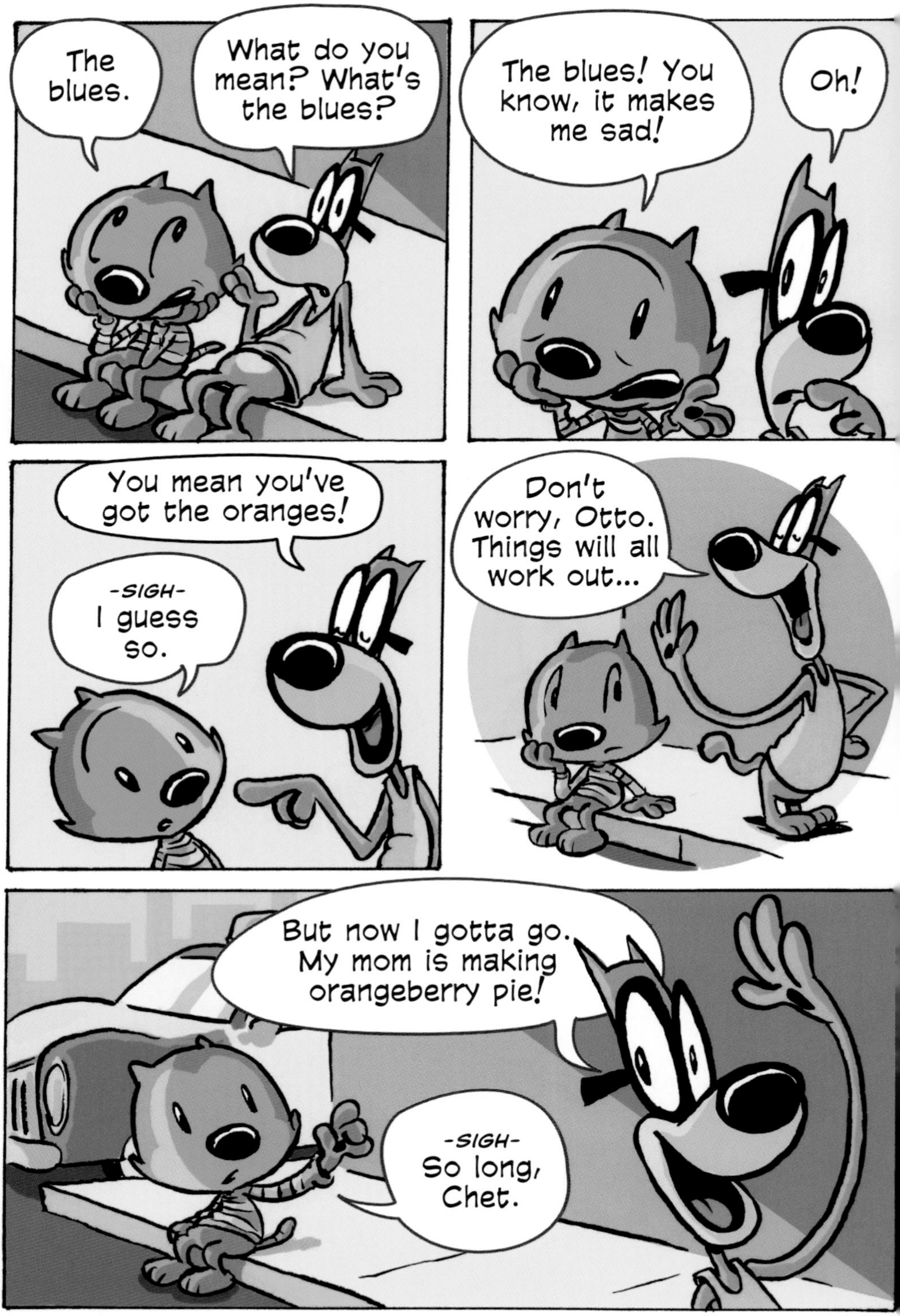
The blues.
What do you mean? What's the blues?
The blues! You know, it makes me sad!
Oh!
You mean you've got the oranges!
-SIGH- I guess so.
Don't worry, Otto. Things will all work out...
But now I gotta go. My mom is making orangeberry pie!
-SIGH- So long, Chet.

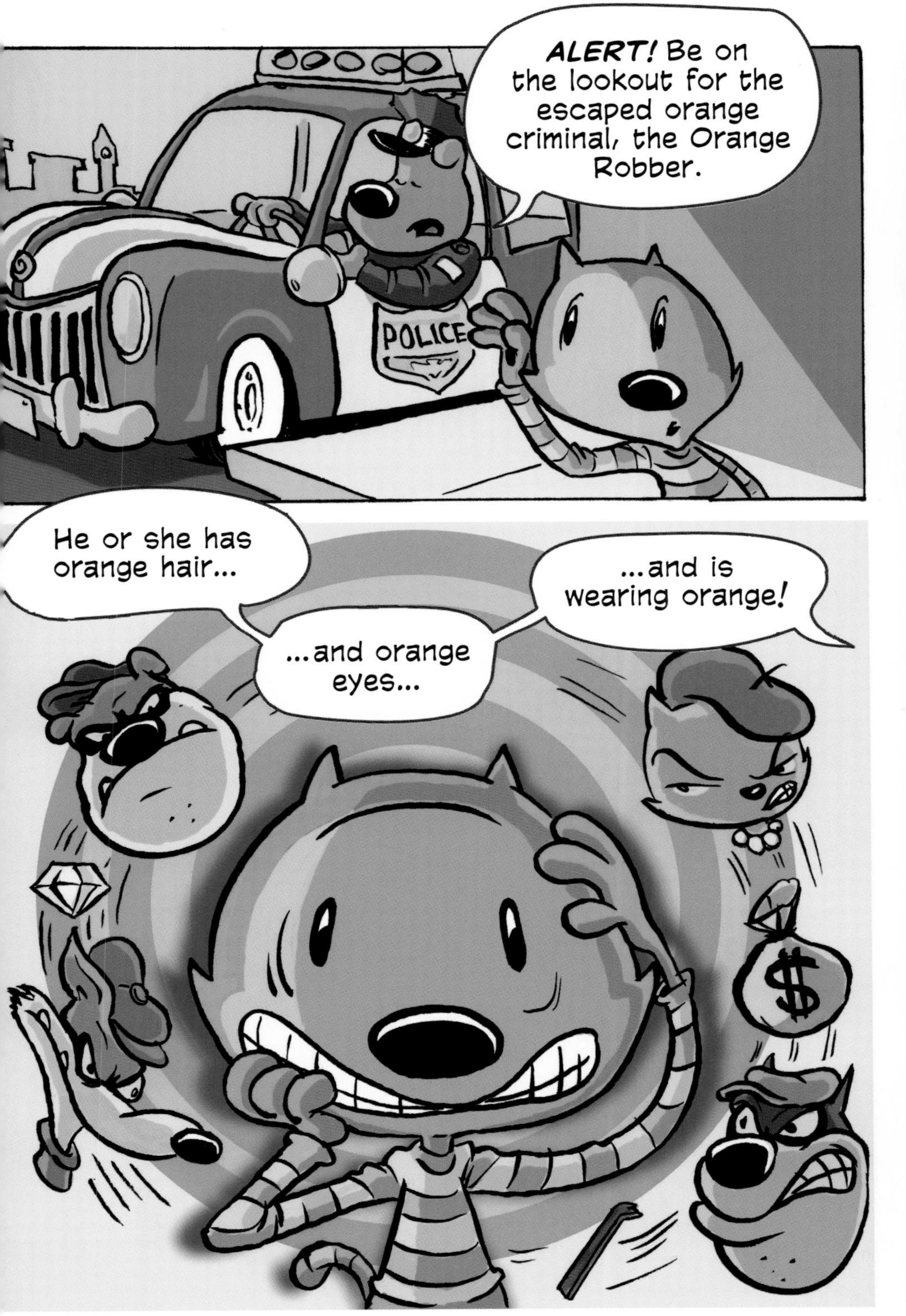
ALERT! Be on the lookout for the escaped orange criminal, the Orange Robber.
POLICE
He or she has orange hair...
...and orange eyes...
...and is wearing orange!

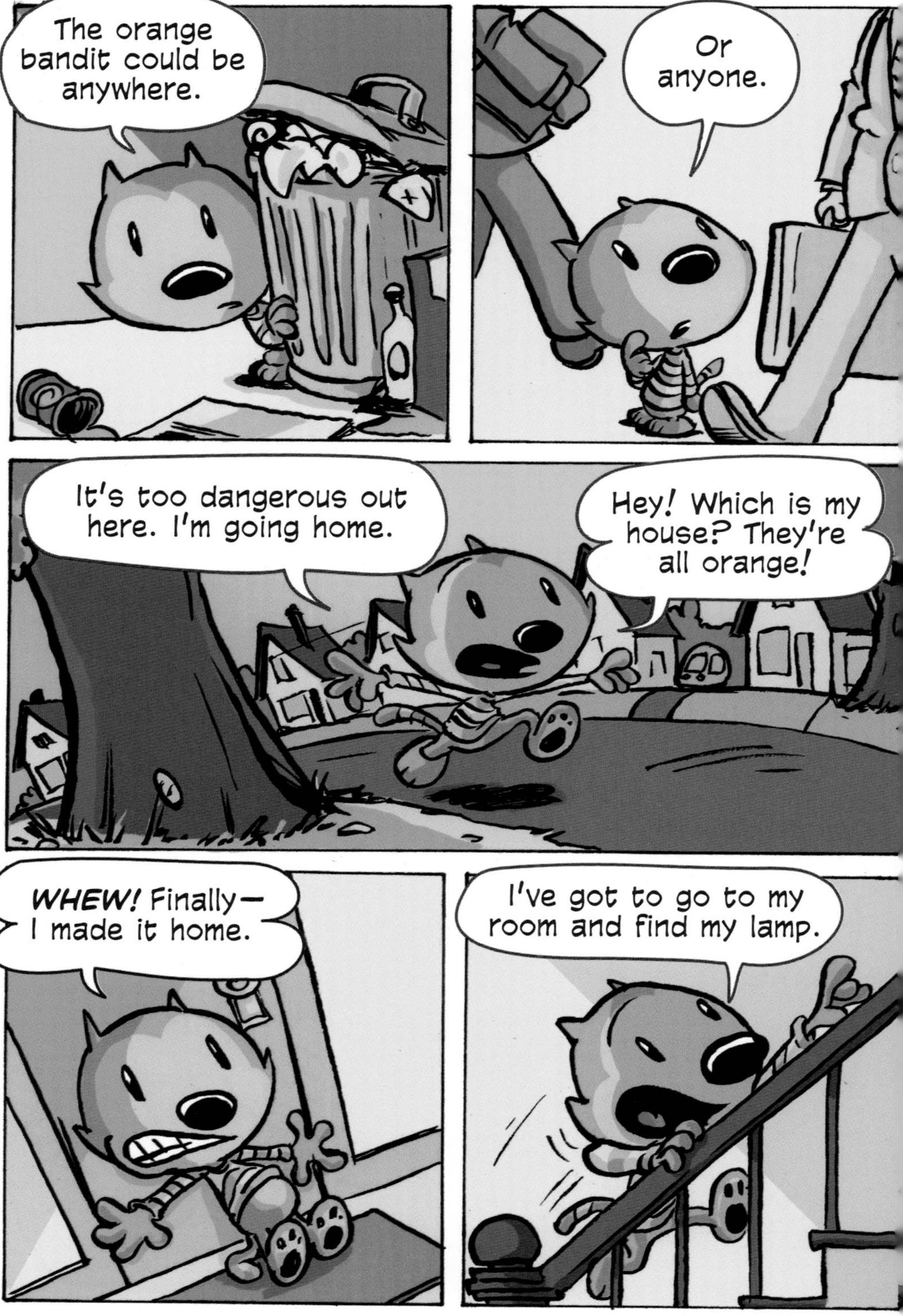
The orange bandit could be anywhere.
Or anyone.
It's too dangerous out here. I'm going home.
Hey! Which is my house? They're all orange!
WHEW! Finally— I made it home.
I've got to go to my room and find my lamp.

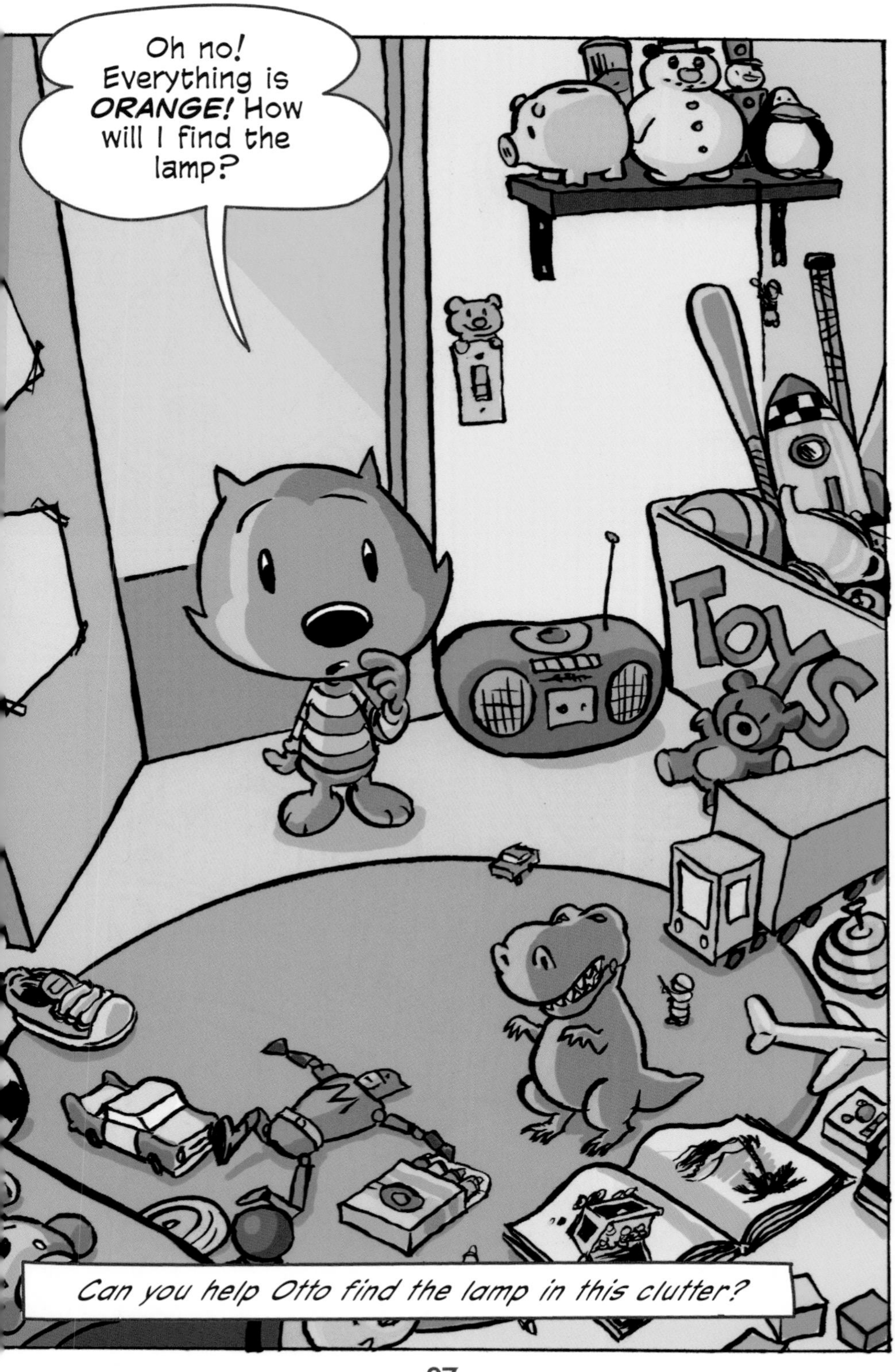
Oh no! Everything is ORANGE! How will I find the lamp?
Toys
Can you help Otto find the lamp in this clutter?

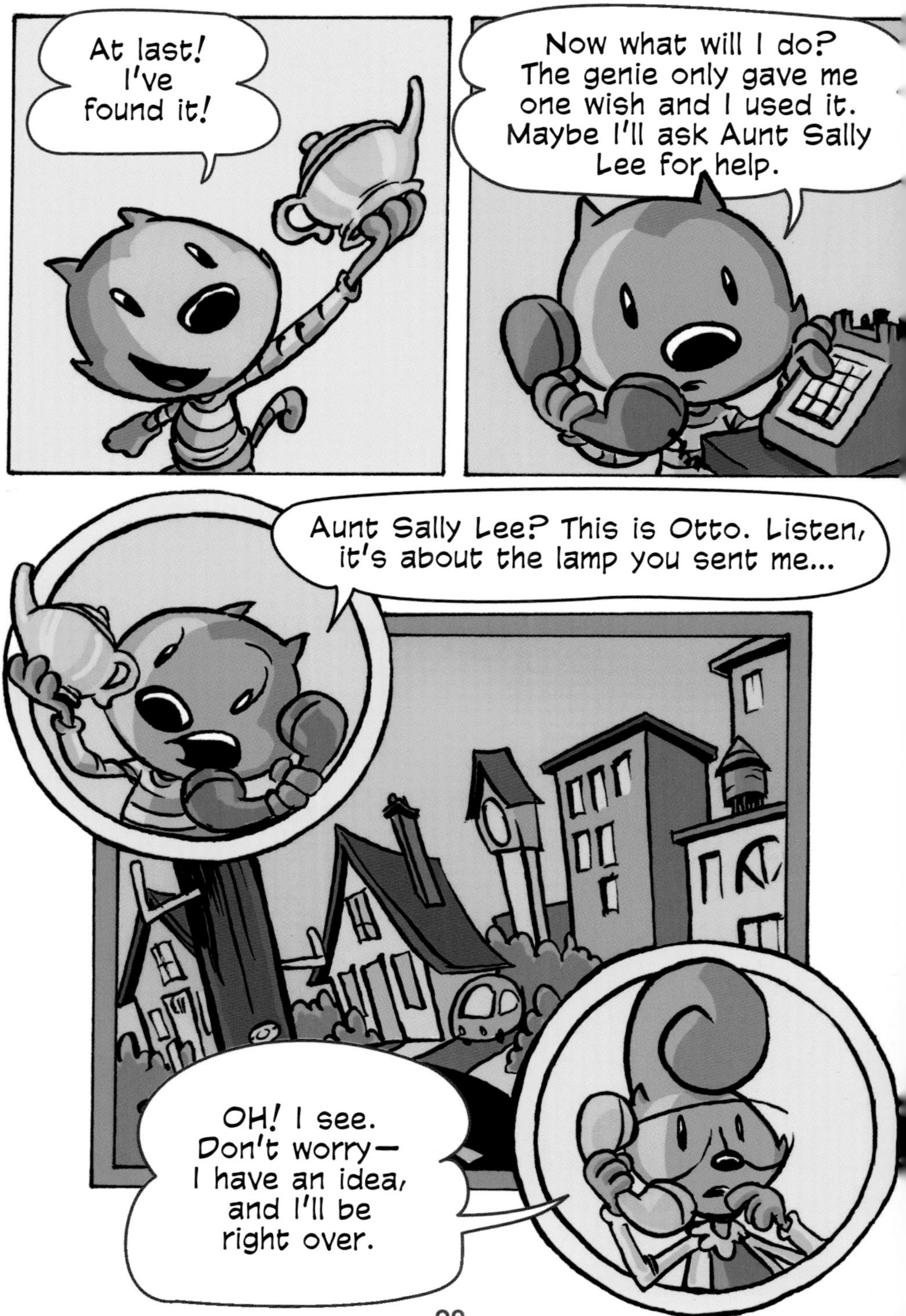
At last! I've found it!
Now what will I do? The genie only gave me one wish and I used it. Maybe I'll ask Aunt Sally Lee for help.
Aunt Sally Lee? This is Otto. Listen, it's about the lamp you sent me...
OH! I see. Don't worry— I have an idea, and I'll be right over.

CHAPTER THREE:

A NEW WISH

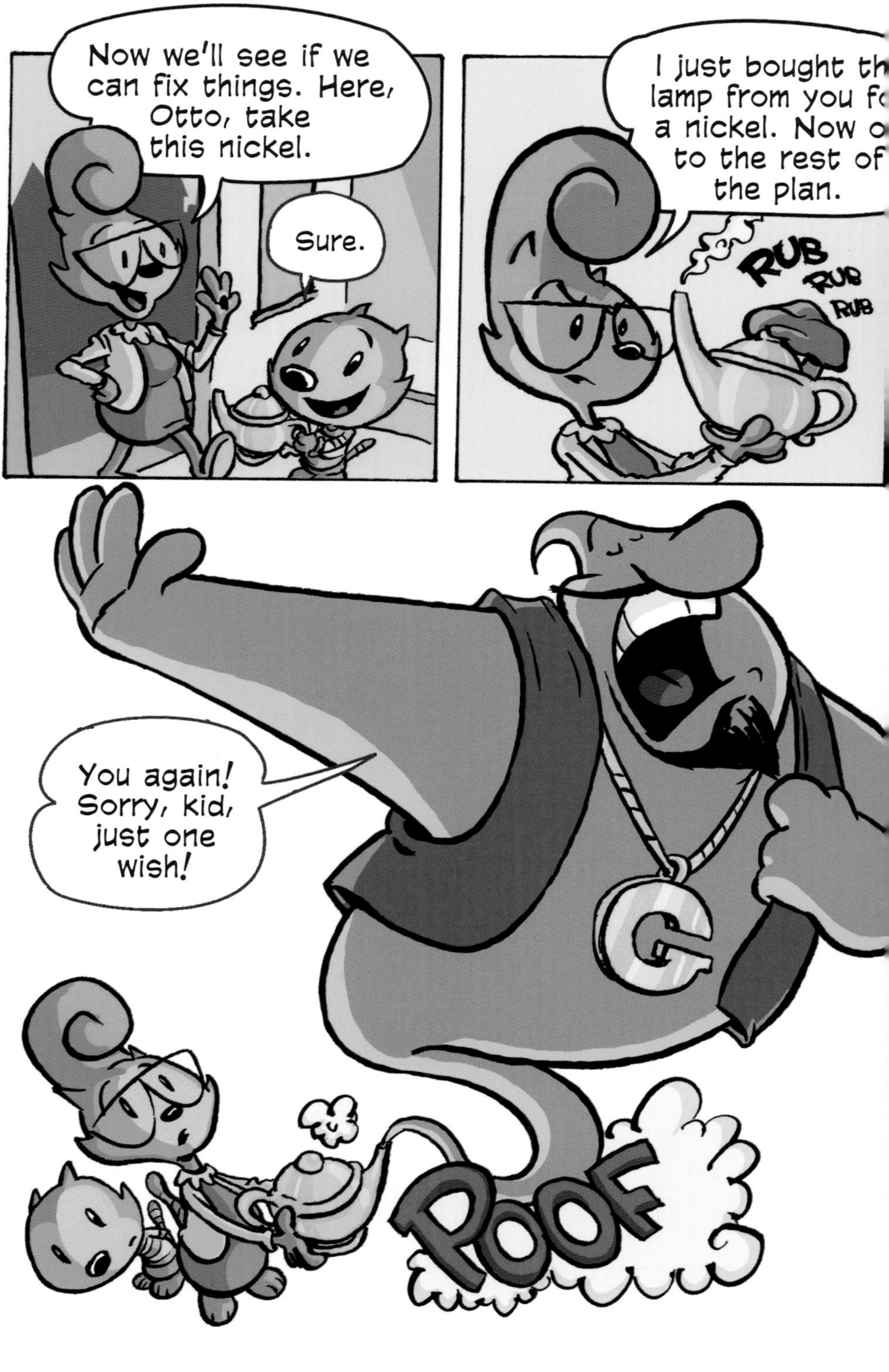
Now we'll see if we can fix things. Here, Otto, take this nickel.
Sure.
I just bought th lamp from you f a nickel. Now o to the rest of the plan.
RUB RUB RUB
You again! Sorry, kid, just one wish!
G
POOF

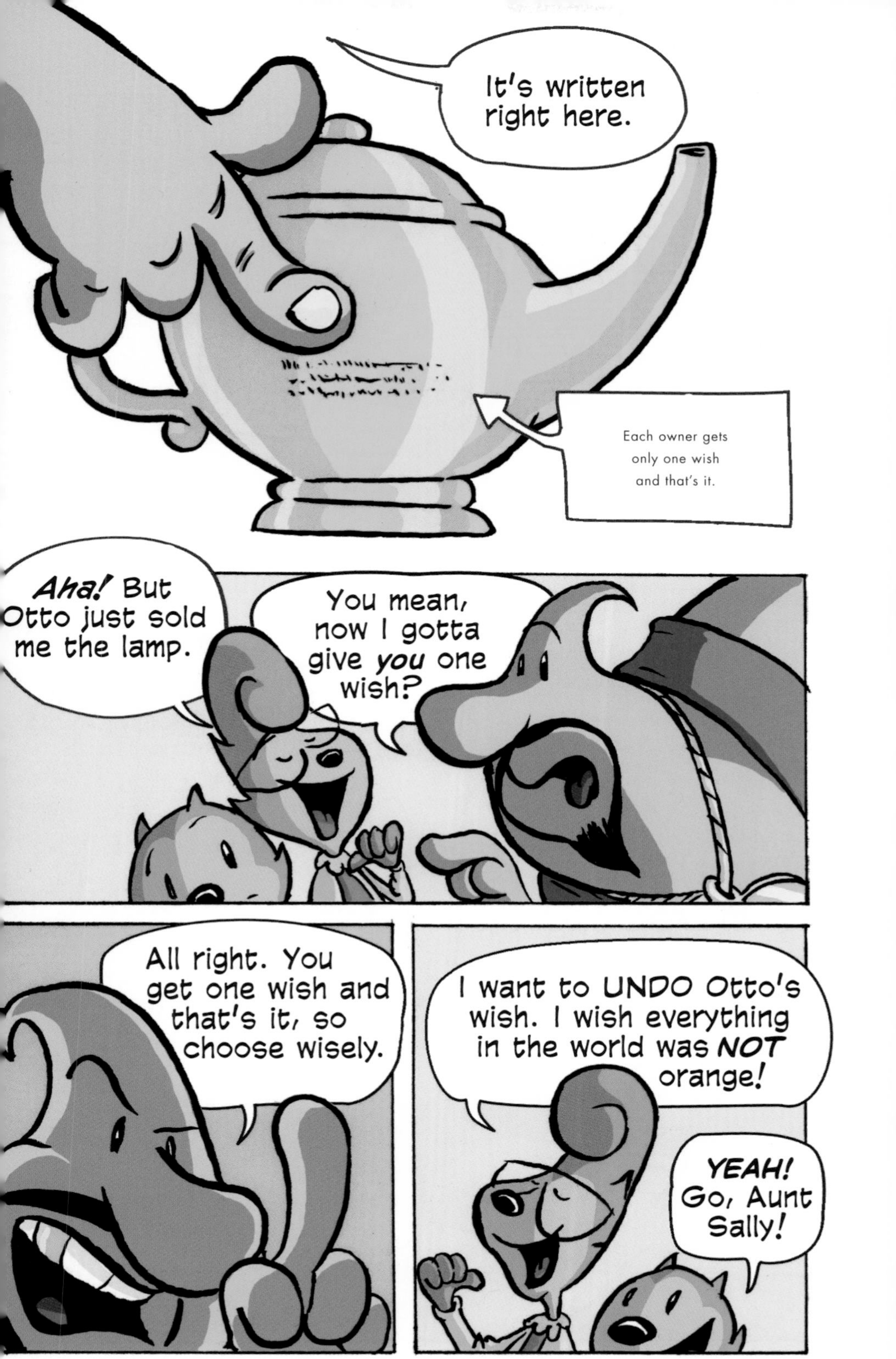
It's written right here.
Each owner gets only one wish and that's it.
Aha! But Otto just sold me the lamp.
You mean, now I gotta give *you* one wish?
All right. You get one wish and that's it, so choose wisely.
I want to UNDO Otto's wish. I wish everything in the world was *NOT* orange!
YEAH! Go, Aunt Sally!

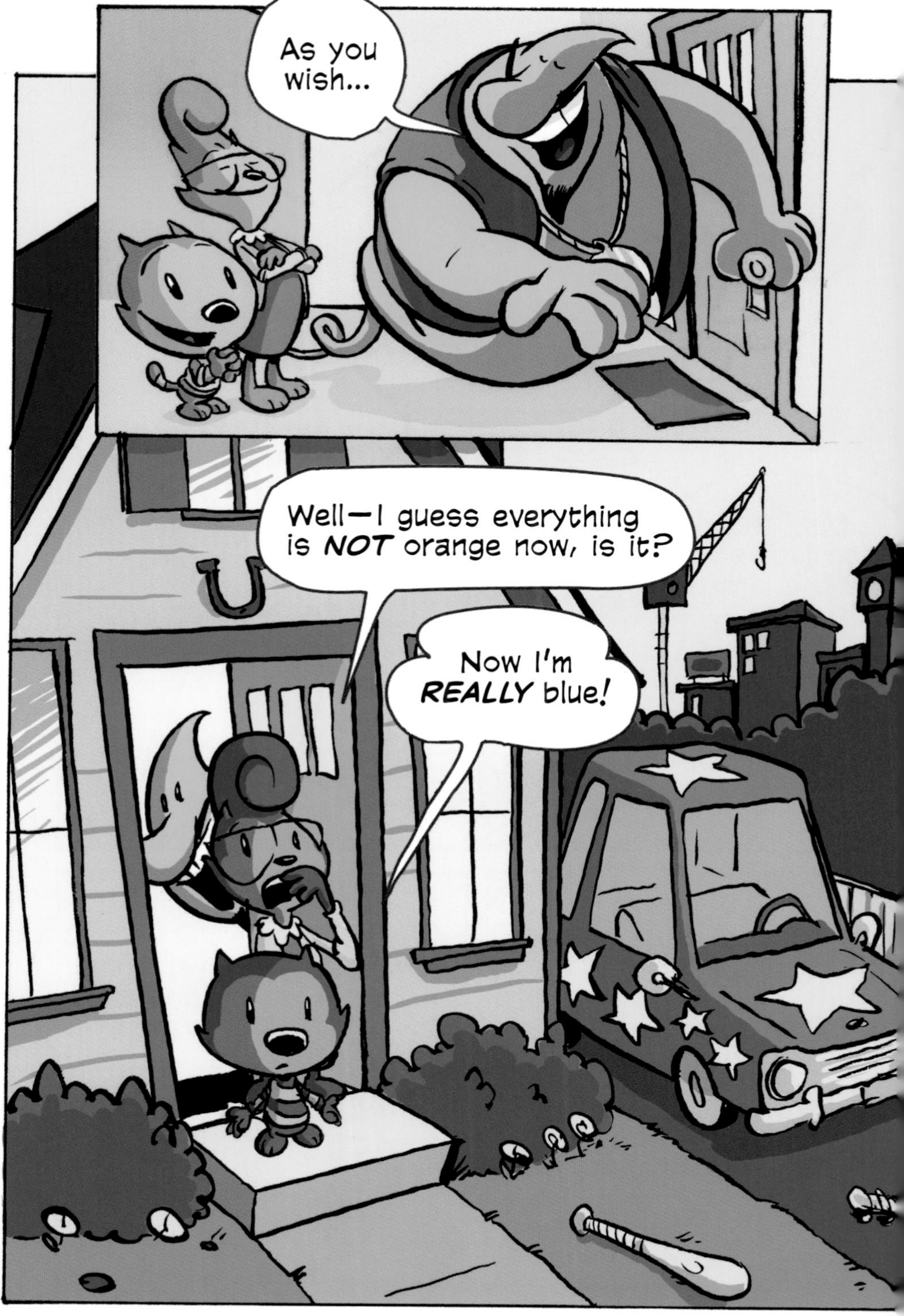
As you wish...
Well—I guess everything is NOT orange now, is it?
Now I'm REALLY blue!

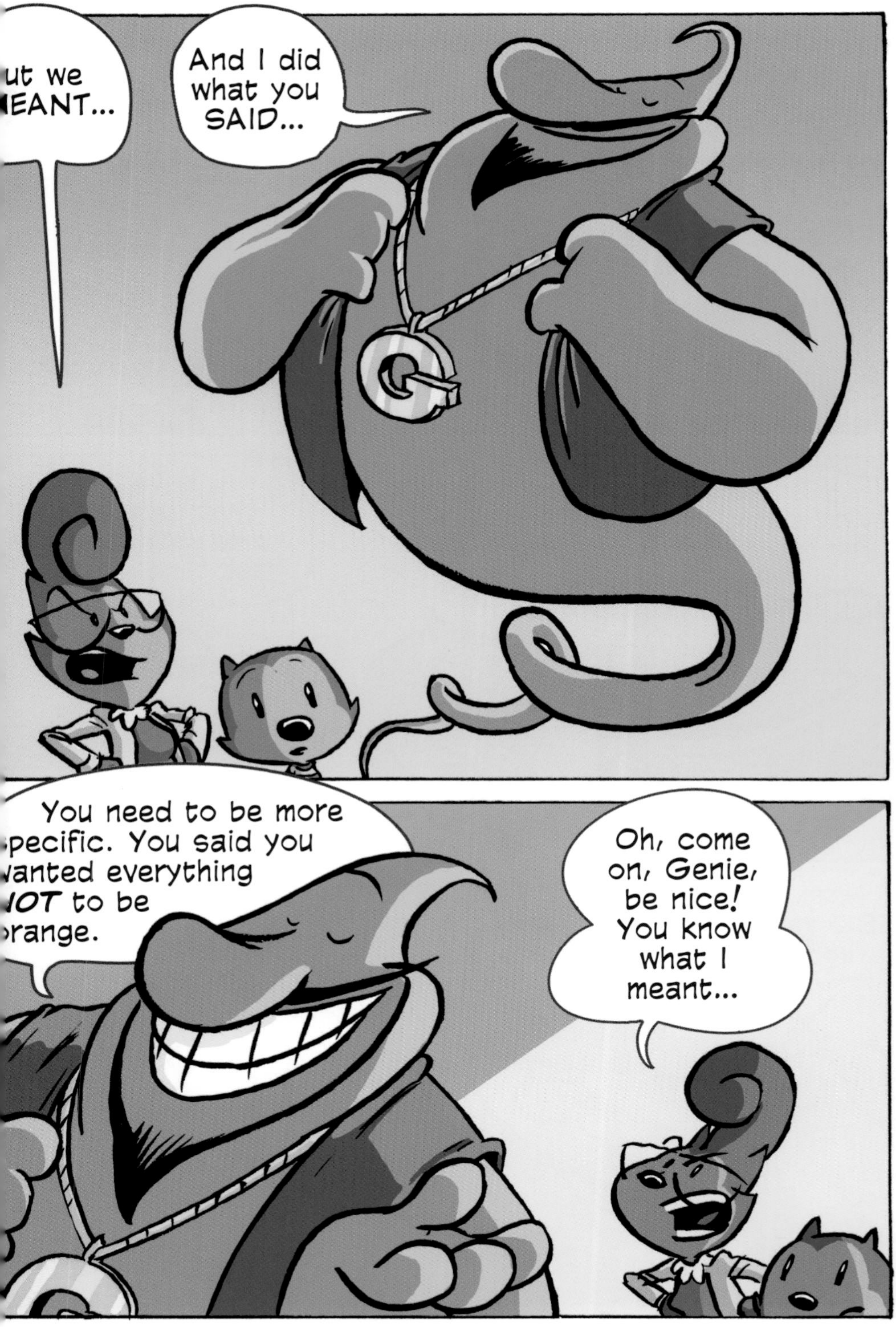
ut we EANT...
And I did what you SAID...
You need to be more pecific. You said you vanted everything *IOT* to be range.
Oh, come on, Genie, be nice! You know what I meant...

34

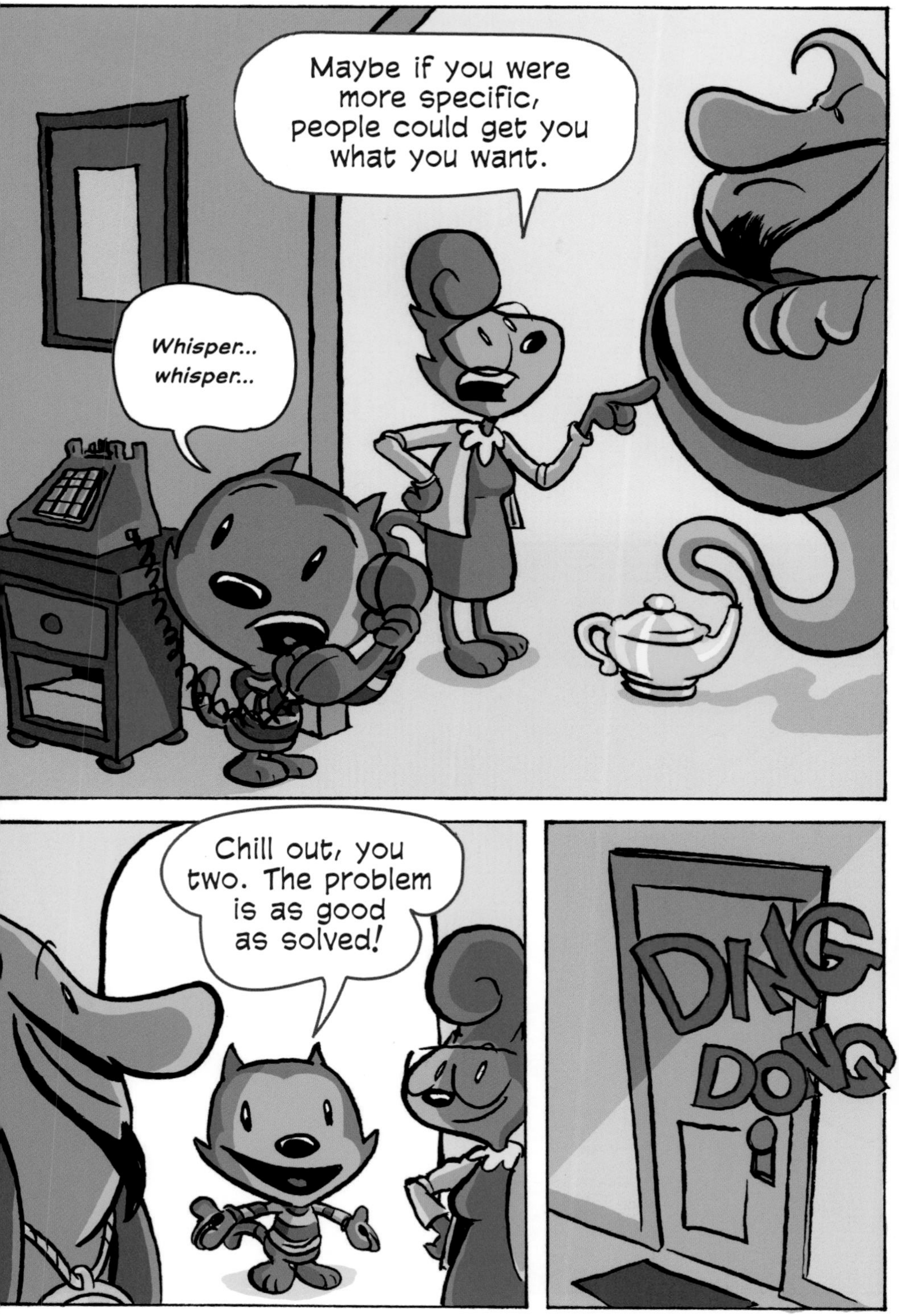
Maybe if you were more specific, people could get you what you want.
Whisper... whisper...
Chill out, you two. The problem is as good as solved!
DING DONG

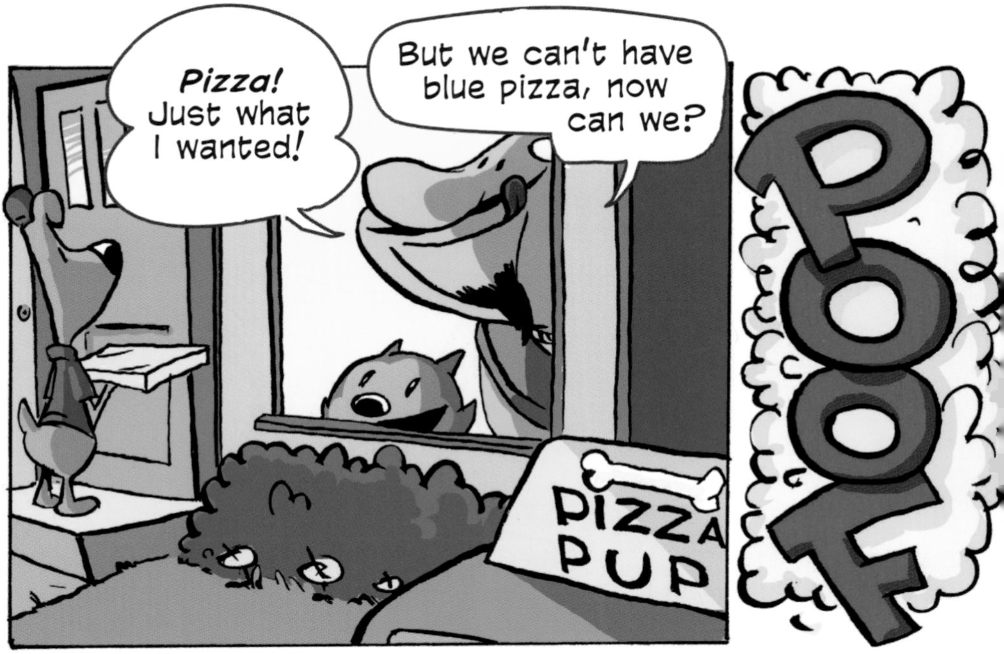
Pizza! Just what I wanted!
But we can't have blue pizza, now can we?
PIZZA PUP
POOF

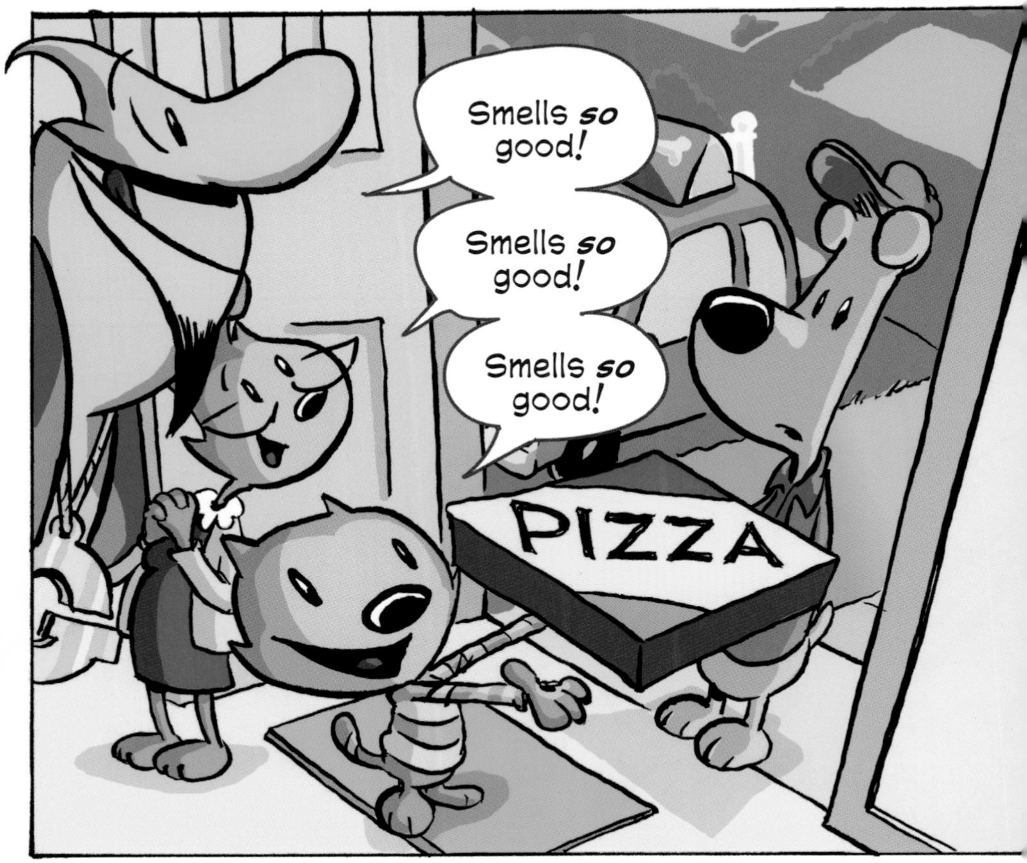
Smells *so* good!
Smells *so* good!
Smells *so* good!
PIZZA

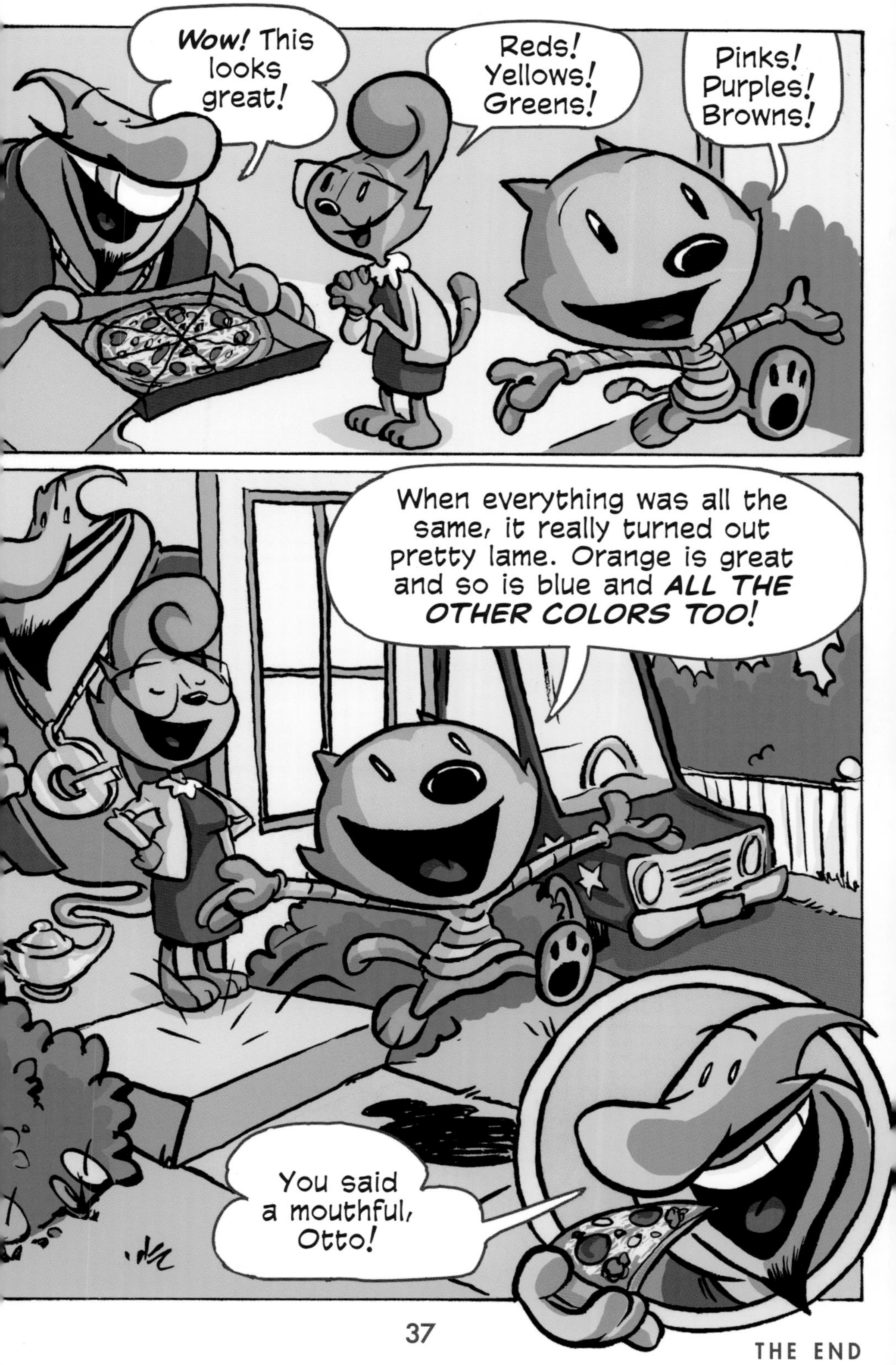

Wow! This looks great!
Reds! Yellows! Greens!
Pinks! Purples! Browns!
When everything was all the same, it really turned out pretty lame. Orange is great and so is blue and ***ALL THE OTHER COLORS TOO!***
You said a mouthful, Otto!

THE END

TOON INTO FUN
at TOON-BOOKS.COM

TOON READERS are a revolutionary online tool that allows all readers to ***TOON INTO READING!***

TOON READERS: you will love hearing the authors read their books when you click the balloons. TOON READERS are also offered in Spanish, French, Russian, Chinese and other languages, a breakthrough for all readers including English Language Learners.

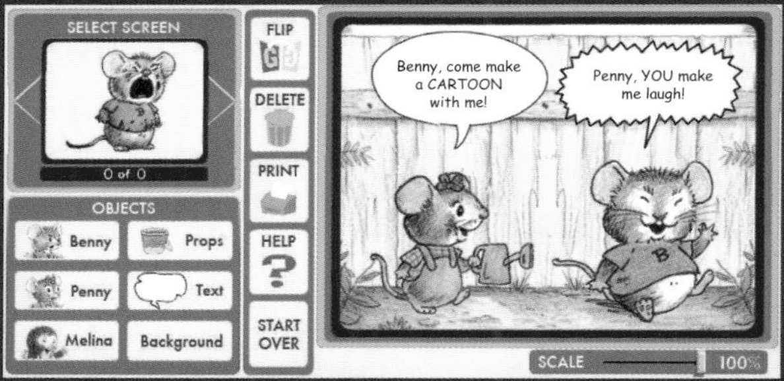
SELECT SCREEN
0 of 0
OBJECTS
Benny
Props
Penny
Text
Melina
Background
FLIP
DELETE
PRINT
HELP
START OVER
Benny, come make a CARTOON with me!
Penny, YOU make me laugh!
SCALE
100%

Young readers are young writers: our **CARTOON MAKER** lets you create your own cartoons with your favorite TOON characters.

And tune into our **KIDS' CARTOON GALLERY**: Send us your cartoons and come read your friends' cartoons. We post the funniest ones online for everyone to see!

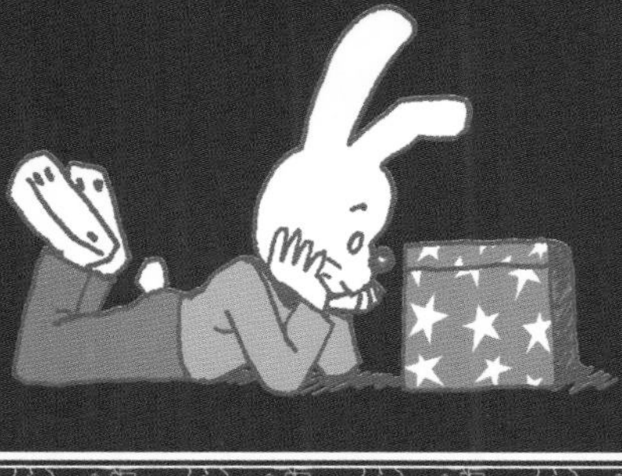

ABOUT THE AUTHORS

JAY LYNCH, who wrote Otto's story, was born in Orange, NJ (honest, ORANGE, NJ!) and now lives in upstate New York. He is the founder of *Bijou Funnies,* one of the first and most important underground comics of the Sixties, and for many years wrote the weekly syndicated comic strip, *Phoebe and the Pigeon People.* He has helped create some of Topps Chewing Gum's most popular humor products, such as *Wacky Packages* and *Garbage Pail Kids,* and has also composed lyrics for the award-winning rock band The Boogers.

FRANK CAMMUSO, who drew Otto's adventure, lives in Syracuse, New York, where he is the award-winning political cartoonist for the *Syracuse Post-Standard.* He is the Eisner-nominated creator of *Max Hamm Fairy Tale Detective,* selected as one of the Top Ten Graphic Novels of 2006 by *Booklist,* and is the author/illustrator of the *Knights of the Lunch Table* series. His writing has appeared in *The New Yorker, The New York Times, The Village Voice,* and *Slate.* His favorite color is red.